The Rain Before It Falls

JONATHAN COE

PENGUIN BOOKS

PENGUIN BOOKS

Published by the Penguin Group
Penguin Books Ltd, 80 Strand, London WC2R ORL, England
Penguin Group (USA) Inc., 375 Hudson Street, New York, New York 10014, USA
Penguin Group (Canada), 90 Eglinton Avenue East, Suite 700, Toronto, Ontario, Canada M4P 2Y3
(a division of Pearson Penguin Canada Inc.)
Penguin Ireland, 25 St Stephen's Green, Dublin 2, Ireland (a division of Penguin Books Ltd)
Penguin Group (Australia), 707 Collins Street, Melbourne, Victoria 3008, Australia
(a division of Pearson Australia Group Pty Ltd)
Penguin Books India Pvt Ltd, 11 Community Centre, Panchsheel Park, New Delhi – 110 017, India
Penguin Group (NZ), 67 Apollo Drive, Rosedale, Auckland 0632, New Zealand
(a division of Pearson New Zealand Ltd)
Penguin Books (South Africa) (Pty) Ltd, Block D, Rosebank Office Park,
181 Jan Smuts Avenue, Parktown North, Gauteng 2193, South Africa

Penguin Books Ltd, Registered Offices: 80 Strand, London WC2R ORL, England

www.penguin.com

First published by Viking 2007
Published in Penguin Books 2008
Reissued in this edition 2014
001

Copyright © Jonathan Coe, 2007

The moral right of the author has been asserted

Printed in Great Britain by Clays Ltd, St Ives plc

A CIP catalogue record for this book is available from the British Library

ISBN: 978-0-241-96775-1

www.greenpenguin.co.uk

Note

The title of this novel comes from a tune by Michael Gibbs. The description of Catharine's music is inspired by the work of Theo Travis on his album *Slow Life*.

When the telephone rang Gill was outside, raking the leaves into coppery piles, while her husband shovelled them on to a bonfire. It was a Sunday afternoon in late autumn. She ran into the kitchen when she heard its shrilling, and immediately felt the warmth of inside enfold her, not having realized, until then, how chilly the air had become. There would most likely be a frost that night.

Afterwards, she walked back up the path towards the little bonfire, from which blue-grey smoke was spiralling into a sky already beginning to darken.

Stephen turned as he heard her approach. He saw bad news in her eyes, and his thoughts flew, at once, to their daughters: to the imagined dangers of central London, to bombs, to once-routine tube and bus journeys suddenly turned into wagers with life and death.

'What is it?'

And when Gill told him that Rosamond had died, finally, at the age of seventy-three, he was unable to ward off a shameful flood of relief. He took Gill in his arms, and they embraced gently, in a silence broken, for a minute or more, only by the crackle of burning leaves, the call of a wood pigeon, the murmur of distantly passing cars.

'The doctor found her,' Gill said, easing away. 'She was sitting up in her armchair, stiff as a board.' She sighed. 'Well, I shall have to go to Shropshire tomorrow and talk to the lawyer. Start fixing up the funeral.'

'Tomorrow? I can't come,' Stephen said quickly.

'I know.'

'It's the trustees' meeting. Everyone will be there. I'm supposed to be chairing.'

'I know. Don't worry.'

She smiled and turned, her ash-blonde hair the only distinct part of her, bobbing down the garden pathway; leaving him, as so often, with a sense of having obscurely failed her.

*

The funeral took place on Friday morning. The village, which Gill remembered from her childhood as being painted-by-numbers in vivid primary colours, was washed grey. The rich blue sky of those memories, still miraculously preserved somewhere on so many hundreds of transparencies, was reduced now to a sheet of perfect white, signifying nothing. Against this featureless backdrop, clusters of sycamore and conifer waved dark green and viridescent in the breeze, the rustle of their leaves the only sound to break in upon the imperishable noise of far-off traffic. In the churchyard itself there stretched a lawn of paler green, broken only intermittently by mossy and lichened outcrops of stone, where headstones rose up unassumingly, or sometimes jutted at curious angles, neglected. Beyond them, in that weak autumnal light, stood the tower of the Church of All Saints: reddish-brown, squat, ageless, the incongruously bright and burnished golden hands on its clock face pointing almost to eleven o'clock. The brickwork was jumbled and irregular, like ecclesiastical crazy paving. Rooks nested on the turreted rooftop.

Gill stood beneath the little wooden porch at the entrance to the churchyard, arm-in-arm with her father, Thomas, watching a steady trickle of mourners rounding the corner past the Fox and Hounds. Her brother David stood beside them. The last time brother and sister had come to this churchyard together, more than twenty years before, it had been to tend the graves of their maternal grandparents, James and Gwendoline. That had been an unsettling visit: Gill was prone (in those days) to clairvoyant episodes, intimations of the supernatural, and afterwards she swore to David that she had seen their grandparents' ghosts: a vision, she claimed, glimpsed only briefly but with absolute clarity, of the two of them sitting on a bench, drinking tea from a Thermos flask and absorbed in sporadic but amicable conversation. David had never known whether to believe her or not, and today, somehow, it seemed tactless to mention the incident. Instead they stood in silent solidarity beside their father and nodded greetings at each new arrival, not recognizing most of them: there were elderly friends of the deceased, and distant relatives, long since forgotten or presumed dead themselves. Few of those assembled seemed to know each other. It was a curiously unsocial gathering.

The service was taken by the Reverend Tawn, whom Gill had met for the first time only that week. During their brief conversations she had found herself liking and trusting him, and although he had not been a close friend of her aunt's, he spoke about her fondly, and well. Then, with the formalities over, a handful of mourners drifted haphazardly back towards the welcoming doors of the pub. Gill watched her father and brother walking down the lane ahead of her: she was, for some reason, inexpressibly touched by the sight of elderly father and middle-aged son walking side by side like this, the relationship between them so evident from their posture, the shapes of their bodies, their whole *way of being* in the world (she could not have put it any more precisely). Would it have been just as obvious to a stranger, she wondered, that the two slender, dark-haired young women trailing a few yards behind her were her own daughters? She turned and glanced at them. They had both inherited their father's looks; but Catharine – temperamental, inward-looking, creative – nonetheless had something of her mother's bearing, her hesitancy and shyness; whereas Elizabeth had always seemed far more grounded and confident, with a sardonic, unflappable humour that would see her through any crisis. Gill could look at them both sometimes and consider them entirely as alien beings; she would find herself baffled

4

to explain how they had ever contrived to pitch up on this planet, let alone in her family. These occasional moments of detachment alarmed her – they felt like panic attacks – but they were fleeting and hallucinatory: all it took for the sensation to slip away was a gesture of closeness from one of her daughters: as now, when Elizabeth suddenly quickened her pace to catch up with her mother, and seized her by the arm.

Even before they had reached the doorway of the public bar, however, Gill disentangled herself from the embrace: she had spotted someone across the car park and needed to speak to her. It was Philippa May, her late aunt's doctor, with whom Gill had been in regular telephone contact over the last few weeks. It was Dr May who had diagnosed Rosamond's heart disease; had tried to persuade her (unsuccessfully) to undergo bypass surgery; had got into the routine of visiting her at home every few days, increasingly concerned about the possibility of a sudden deterioration; and finally, last Sunday morning, had arrived at the house to find the back door unlocked, and Rosamond's body recumbent upon the armchair in which – by the looks of things – she had passed away at least twelve hours earlier.

'Philippa!' Gill called as she hurried over.

On the point of getting into her car, Dr May straightened up and turned. She was a small, efficient woman, with unruly grey hair and warm, confidence-inspiring blue eyes which glinted out from behind an old-fashioned pair of steel-rimmed spectacles.

'Oh, hello, Gill. What a wretched business this is. I'm so very sorry.'

'You can't stay for a few minutes?'

'I would have liked to, but . . .'

'Of course. Well, I just wanted to say thank you, for everything you've done. She was lucky to have you – as a friend and a doctor.'

Dr May smiled doubtfully, as if unused to receiving compliments. 'I'm afraid you've got a lot of work ahead of you,' she said. 'That house was full of clutter.'

'I can imagine,' said Gill. 'I haven't been there yet. I've been putting it off.'

'Well, I tried not to disturb anything. There were one or two adjustments I took the liberty of making. The record player needed to be turned off, for one thing.'

'Record player?'

'Yes. She seems to have been listening to music when it happened. Quite a comforting thought, in my opinion. There was a record still going round on the turntable when I got there. The needle was stuck in a groove at the end of one side.' She reflected briefly; and, although the tendency of her thoughts was clearly morbid, at that moment, she almost managed a smile. 'In fact, I wondered at first if she'd been singing along, when I saw the microphone in her hand.'

Gill stared at her. This was quite the most surprising thing she had heard all week. Images of Aunt

Rosamond brightening up her last minutes by staging an impromptu karaoke session fled through her mind.

'It was connected to an old cassette recorder,' Dr May explained. 'A very old cassette recorder, I should say. 1970s vintage. The "record" button was still pressed down.'

Gill frowned. 'What would she have been recording, I wonder?'

The doctor shook her head. 'I don't know: but there was a whole pile of tapes there. Photograph albums, too. Well, you'll see it all soon enough. Everything should be just as I left it.'

*

The drive home to Oxfordshire took more than two hours. Gill had been worried that both her daughters would want to travel straight on to London; but they surprised and delighted her by asking if they could stay the whole weekend. That evening they had what was, by the household's normal standards, a noisy family dinner together; and after that, once Thomas had gone to bed, they fell to discussing the unexpected provisions of Rosamond's will.

Rosamond had left no children. Her longtime companion – a woman called Ruth – had died some time ago, back in the 1990s. Her sister Sylvia was also dead, and there was no bequest to her brother-in-law Thomas. ('You're not disappointed, are you, Grandpa?' Catharine had asked him that night, sitting at the end of his bed in the self-contained annexe which he had lately, and reluctantly, learned to regard as his home. Thomas shook his head, dismissing the idea. 'I asked her not to,' he said. 'What would be the point?' Catharine smiled and squeezed his hand and turned the radio on before she left. She knew that he always liked to listen to the news at eleven o'clock, checking up on the world – tucking it in – before he fell asleep.) Instead, Rosamond had divided her estate three ways: one-third each to her niece and nephew, Gill and David, and the remaining third to a stranger; a near-stranger, anyway, as far as they were concerned. Her name was Imogen, and Gill had no idea where she was to be found these days, having met her only once, more than twenty years ago.

'I suppose Imogen would be getting on for thirty now,' Gill said, as Catharine refilled her glass with a deep red Merlot, and Stephen stirred the fire back into flame. All four of them were circled around the hearth; Stephen and Gill in armchairs, their daughters sitting cross-legged between them on the floor. 'The only time I ever saw her was at Rosamond's birthday party – her fiftieth, that would have been – and then she can't have been more than seven or eight years old. She was there all by herself. I talked to her for quite a while . . .'

'She came all by herself?' Catharine prompted, but her mother didn't seem to hear. She was thinking what a strange party that had been. Not in Shropshire, this time. No, this was a few years before Rosamond had retired, once and for all, to the beloved county of her wartime childhood. In those days, she and Ruth had been living in London, in a substantial terraced villa, somewhere like Belsize Park. It was a foreign country, to Gill and her family. For the first time in her life, she had felt acutely provincial, and saw her parents in the same light. She had watched as her mother and Rosamond exchanged awkward, halting greetings in the basement kitchen ('Fancy having a kitchen in the basement!' Sylvia had marvelled afterwards) and wondered how it was possible for two sisters to be so distant, even with almost ten years between them. And while few situations ever seemed to disconcert her father, who was, apart from anything else, the most widely travelled member of the family, even he seemed ill at ease on this occasion: still handsome, then, in his late fifties, with full silvery hair and a complexion only just beginning to verge upon the florid, he had spent most of the afternoon examining the bookshelves before settling down in an armchair with a tumbler of whisky and a recently published history of the Baltic States.

As for Gill herself, she had stood alone (why was Stephen not there?) for what seemed like hours on the steps leading down to the tiny garden ('You're so lucky,' she had heard someone say to Aunt Rosamond, 'having such a big garden in this part of town'), leaning against the wrought-iron rail and watching the ebb and flow of exotic guests as they drifted in and out of the house. (Why had so few of them come to the funeral?)

She could remember feeling angry with herself: angry at the thought that she was now in her mid-twenties, had been through university, was already married (and not only married, but three months pregnant with Catharine), and yet here she was, feeling as gauche and shy as any teenager, utterly incapable of striking up a conversation. Her wine glass was growing warm and sticky in her hands, and she was on the point of going inside to refill it when Imogen came out through the French windows behind her. She was being led by Aunt Rosamond, who was holding her gently but firmly by the upper arm.

'This way, this way,' Rosamond was saying. 'There are lots of people out here for you to talk to.'

They stopped beside Gill on the top step, and Imogen reached out a tentative hand. Instinctively, without quite knowing why she was helping her in this way, Gill took hold of the hand and laid it on the railing for her. Imogen gripped the railing solidly.

'This,' said Rosamond to the little girl, 'is Gill, my niece. You might not be aware of it, but Gill is also one of your relations. You are cousins. Second cousins once removed, if that means anything to you. And she has come a long way to see me today, just like you. Aren't I lucky, to have so many people come to visit me on my birthday? Gill, are you enjoying yourself? Would you like to take Imogen down into the garden for a moment? Only she's a little bit lost, with all these people, I think.'

Imogen was very fair, and very quiet. She had a strong, prominent jaw, three missing baby teeth with gaps where the new ones had not yet come through, and her blonde hair fell in a tangle over her eyes. Gill would not have guessed that she was blind, had Rosamond not whispered the information to her before she turned and disappeared indoors. When her aunt had gone, Gill looked down and stroked the little girl's hair.

'Come with me,' she said.

*

They had all fallen in love with Imogen that afternoon. She was almost twenty years younger than anybody else at the party, which of course already made her the focus of adoring attention; but beyond that, the very fact of her blindness seemed to draw the other guests to her. They were drawn through sympathy, at first, and then by the strange quality of stillness, of centredness, that seemed to surround the small, fair-haired child. She was very calm, and the half-smile upon her face appeared to be permanent. Her voice, on the rare occasions when she spoke, was almost inaudibly gentle.

'How funny,' Gill had said, 'to think that we're related, and we've never met before.'

'I don't live with my mother,' said Imogen. 'I have another family.'

'Didn't they come with you today?' Gill asked, looking around her.

'We all came down to London together. But they didn't want to come to the party.'

'Well, don't worry. I'll look after you for a bit.'

Later that afternoon, Gill had taken Imogen upstairs to the toilet and then stood waiting for her on the landing near by. Soon Imogen found her again and took her hand and asked: 'What are you looking at?'

'Oh, I was just looking at the view. You get a good view from up here.'

'What can you see?'

'You can see ...' But for a few moments Gill didn't know where to begin. All she could see, in fact, was the formlessness of jumbled buildings, trees, skyline. It struck her that this was as much as she ever saw. But she could not describe it to Imogen in those terms. She would have to look at it in an entirely new way, piece by piece, item by item. And start ... with what? The haze which blurred the line of transition from rooftops to sky? The sky's barely perceptible gradations of colour, from the deepest to the palest of blues? The weird collision of outlines where two tower blocks stood on either side of what she took to be St Paul's Cathedral?

'Well,' she began, 'the sky is blue and the sun is shining ...'

'I know that, silly,' said Imogen, and squeezed Gill's hand.

And even now Gill could remember it, so clearly, the pressure of those tiny fingers. Her first intimation of what it would be like, to have a daughter of her own. At that moment she had clutched to herself the knowledge that Catharine was growing inside her, and felt that she could hardly tolerate the fear and gladness.

★

Thomas, as usual, was the first to wake up next morning. Gill made him some tea, poached a couple of eggs, then left her father reading the newspaper while she fetched twenty or so boxes of Kodak slides from the lower reaches of the old mahogany bureau in the study, and took them into the dining room, where there was more sunlight. She spread them out on the table and tutted when she noticed that most of the boxes were unlabelled. The task of sifting through them more or less methodically took almost half an hour, and when Elizabeth came to join her, dressing-gowned and tousle-haired, she had only just found what she was looking for.

'What's up?' her daughter asked.

'I was trying to find a picture. Of Imogen. Here, look.'

She handed Elizabeth one of the transparencies. Elizabeth held it up to the window and squinted.

'Oh my God,' she said. 'When was this taken?'

'1983. Why?'

'The clothes! The hairstyles! What were you thinking of?'

'Never mind that. Your children will be saying the same thing about you in twenty years' time. This is the party I was telling you about. Rosamond's fiftieth. Can you see her, and Ruth, and me and Grandma?'

'Yes. Where's Grandpa?'

'He must have taken the picture. We'll go and ask him in a minute, see if he remembers. Now – you see the little girl standing in front of Aunt Rosamond?'

Elizabeth held the picture up to a patch of brighter light at the top of the window. Her attention was drawn, at this moment, not to Imogen but to the infinitely strange, infinitely familiar figure standing at the far left of the grouping: this ghostly projection of her mother's younger self. It was what people might have called a 'good photograph', in the sense that it made Gill look attractive, beautiful even. (She had never thought of her mother as beautiful before.) But Elizabeth wished that it told her more than that: wished that it could tell her what her mother might have been thinking, or feeling, at this momentous family party, so soon after her marriage, so newly pregnant. Why did photographs – family photographs – make everyone appear so unreadable? What hopes, what secret anxieties lay behind that seemingly confident tilt of her mother's face, her mouth slipping into its characteristic, slightly crooked smile?

'Yes, I see her,' Elizabeth said, finally, turning her attention back to the little fair-haired girl. 'She looks pretty.'

'Well, that's Imogen. That's who we've got to find.'

'Shouldn't be difficult. You can find anybody, these days.'

To Gill this sounded over-confident; but Catharine, when she joined them at the breakfast table soon afterwards, agreed with her sister. Neither of them was much impressed with the solicitor's plan of action, which was to place an advertisement in *The Times*. Catharine thought this was ludicrous – 'We're not living in the 1950s, and besides, nobody reads *The Times* any more, do they?' ('Least of all a blind person,' Elizabeth added) – and offered to start searching on the internet at once. By ten o'clock, she had presented her mother with a list of five possible candidates.

Gill drafted a letter that afternoon, posted five copies on Monday morning, and then settled down to the uncertain wait for a reply.

*

Meanwhile, she decided that there was no point in deferring the task of visiting Rosamond's house, sorting through her effects and putting it up for sale. It would no doubt be a tiring and complicated process. Having divined, from his silences, that Stephen wanted to have nothing to do with it, she braced herself for three or four days alone in Shropshire, packed a small suitcase and drove back there on a bright, windy and ice-cold Tuesday morning.

Her late aunt's house was hidden off one of the many mud-encrusted lanes which lay between Much Wenlock and Shrewsbury. The approach always managed to take Gill by surprise. Dense banks of rhododendron announced that you were nearly there, for behind them, she knew, stretched Rosamond's shady, sequestered garden; but after that, the driveway slyly declined to reveal itself, and instead sidled out on to the carriageway at a preposterous angle which only the smallest car could turn without involving itself in awkward pirouettes and reversals. Once you had found this driveway, it soon narrowed to a rough, pebbly track, and the trees on either side closed in and entwined their serpentine branches overhead until it felt as though you were passing through a vegetable tunnel. Emerging, at last, blinking, into the autumn sunshine, you expected to see at the very least some crumbled baronial hall; but what you found was a modest grey bungalow, built some time in the 1920s or '30s, with a greenhouse leaning up against one side and an air of absolute quiescence which could be quite unnerving. This had always appeared to be the main feature of the house, from the outside, even when Rosamond was alive and now, in the knowledge of her final absence, Gill stepped out of her car that frozen morning to be enveloped at once in a loneliness more complete than any she could remember.

If the silence of the house and its grounds seemed almost unearthly, the cold inside was even worse. Gill could tell, without being morbid or fanciful, that it was more than a question of room temperature. This was a dead person's house. Nothing could take the chill off it: no matter how many radiators she turned on, boilers she fired up, fan heaters she retrieved from forgotten cupboards. She resigned herself to the idea that she would have to work with her coat on.

Gill drifted into the kitchen and looked around her. The sink was full of cold washing-up water: on the draining board a knife and fork, a single plate, two saucepans and a wooden spoon had been laid out to dry. These relics of Rosamond's final hours made her feel sadder than ever. More cheeringly, she saw a coffee-making machine and, standing in readiness next to it, still vacuum-sealed, a packet of fresh Colombia roast. At once she broke it open and brewed up a generous helping, and even before she had taken her first few sips, she felt revived by the companionable noises of bubbling and frothing, and the rich, walnutty fumes that filled the kitchen with aromatic warmth.

She took her mug with her into the sitting room. It was lighter and airier than the kitchen: French windows looked out over a pretty but overgrown stretch of lawn, and Rosamond's armchair had been placed to take advantage of this view. Around the chair, just as Dr May had informed her, were stacked a number of photograph albums – some recent, some almost antique – along with three or four plastic boxes containing transparencies and a small battery-powered device for viewing them. There was something else, too, which gave Gill a jolt of recognition when she noticed it leaning up against the chair: an unframed oil painting, a portrait of the young Imogen, which she had certainly seen somewhere before. (Perhaps – though she could not be sure of this – at Rosamond's house in London, at the fiftieth birthday party?) On the little table next to the chair was a tape recorder, a small microphone – the connecting wire now neatly coiled up and tied around itself – and four cassette jewel cases, standing in an orderly pile. Gill examined these curiously. There were no inlay cards describing the contents, and there was nothing written on the tapes themselves: all she could see were the numbers one to four, which Rosamond appeared to have cut out of cardboard, and then glued, in sequence, to the plastic cases. Furthermore, one of the cases was empty: or rather, instead of housing a tape, all it contained was a sheet of A5 airmail paper, folded up tightly, upon which Rosamond had scrawled the words:

> *Gill —*
> *These are for Imogen.*
> *If you cannot find her, listen to them yourself.*

Where, then, was the fourth tape to be found? In the machine itself, probably. She pressed the eject button and, sure enough, there was another cassette inside. It appeared to match the others, so Gill slipped it into the empty case and took all four of them over to a writing desk which stood in the corner of the room. She wanted to put these tapes out of temptation's way, immediately. In the writing desk she found a large manila envelope; she dropped the tapes into it, sealed the envelope with a couple of quick, decisive licks, and wrote 'Imogen' on the front in capital letters.

Next, Gill went over to the record player, which sat on top of a stained and weathered rosewood cabinet. Again, just as Dr May had told her, there was a record still resting on the turntable. She raised the perspex lid, carefully lifted the record – taking care not to touch the surface – and examined the label. *Songs of the Auvergne*, it said: arranged by Joseph Canteloube, sung by Victoria de los Angeles. Looking around, Gill saw both the sleeve and the inner sleeve lying on a nearby shelf. She put the album back in its sleeve and knelt down to open the cabinet, guessing that Rosamond would have kept her records there. There were about a hundred of them, neatly alphabetized. No CDs, however: the digital revolution seemed to have passed her by. But there were also, on the top shelf of the cabinet, a few dozen more cassettes, some blank and some pre-recorded, and standing next to them, something else, something quite unexpected – enough to make Gill draw in her breath sharply, so that her gasp rang out in that silent house like a scream of distress.

A glass tumbler: just a few drops of liquid at the bottom, giving off the unmistakably peaty smell of an Islay malt whisky. And next to it, a small brown bottle, the contents of which were spelled out on a label in feeble dot-matrix printing: Diazepam. The bottle was empty.

*

At three o'clock in the afternoon, Gill phoned her brother.

'How's it going?' he asked, cheerfully.

'It's miserable here. I can't stand it. How did *she* stand it, for heaven's sake? I'm sorry, but there's no way I'm going to spend the night in this place.'

'So what are you going to do? Drive home?'

'I can't face it. It's too far. Stephen's away in Germany till Friday anyway. I . . .' (she hesitated) '. . . I was wondering if I could stay the night at yours.'

'Of course you could.'

*

No, she would not tell anyone. She had made up her mind about that, now. What she had seen in that cupboard was not conclusive, after all. Perhaps that bottle had been there for months, years. Dr May had expressed herself satisfied as to the cause of death, and had seen no need to refer it to the coroner. Why upset things, then, why cause anyone any needless distress? And even if Rosamond had taken her own life, what business was it of Gill's, or anyone else's? She had known that the end was not far away; the angina had been causing her pain; and if she had chosen to release herself from that pain, who could blame her?

Gill was doing the right thing: she was quite sure of it.

David's house was in Stafford, little more than an hour away. The last few minutes of daylight found her driving through the eastern parts of Shropshire, towards the M6. The route took her not far from the church where Rosamond was now buried, but Gill had no desire to stop. She entered a sort of trance-like state, and drove slowly, never faster than forty miles an hour, unaware that impatient cars were queued up behind her. Her thoughts were drifting randomly, dangerously, floating and untethered. That music her aunt must have been listening to, when she died ... Gill had never heard Canteloube's *Songs of the Auvergne*, but she had visited that part of France herself, once, many years ago. Catharine had been eight years old, Elizabeth five or six, so it must have been 1992: quite early that year – April or May ... The girls had not come with them on that trip, anyway. The whole idea had been to leave them behind, staying with their grandparents. Gill and Stephen had stumbled into a crisis in their marriage (was that putting it too strongly? She remembered no arguments, no infidelities, just a sort of wordless distance opening up between them, a sudden, bewildered awareness that somehow, without anybody noticing, they had become strangers to one another) and their hope, presumably, had been that a few days in France together might help repair the damage.

It hadn't worked that way. Stephen was being flown to Clermont-Ferrand for a conference, and his days were entirely spoken for. Gill had been left to wander alone for hours through the bars and sitting rooms of their empty, newly built, characterless hotel, until she had finally decided, on the third day, to assert her independence. This had involved hiring a car and

21

driving out into the countryside. She retained only a few hazy memories – grey skies, an unexpectedly rocky landscape, a desolate lake surrounded by pine trees – and one other, very clear one: something she had not forgotten in all the intervening years. She had been driving back to the hotel, towards the end of the day; it was late afternoon, and the road she had chosen was narrow, winding, hemmed in by patches of densely planted and rather sinister woodland. Rain was falling in fits and starts, thinly and unpredictably. And then, as the forest at last fell away and Gill emerged on to an open road that was almost eerily flat and lunar, there had been a loud, sudden thud on her windscreen. A black shape bounced off it, then on to the car bonnet and then on to the road, where it lay unmoving. Gill braked to a halt in the middle of the road, ran back to see what the shape was, and found herself looking at a dark blot upon the asphalt – a dead bird, a young blackbird. And on the instant of seeing that lifeless shape another thud fell, leaden, upon her heart. She had turned off the car engine, so that the hush upon the road was now oppressive and shocking. No birdsong anywhere. Gill approached the dead object almost on tiptoe, picked up the small body gingerly, by the edge of one wing, and then placed it gently on a bed of moss under the branches of a lone shrub at the roadside, thinking to herself as she did so, 'You know what it's supposed to mean: a death in the family.' The thought, unbidden and treacherous, caused her heart to start racing, and she drove at reckless speed into the next village, the village of Murol, where, upon finding a callbox, she jammed a handful of francs into the slot as fast as she could and telephoned her parents' house in England. Her mother came to the phone after what seemed like a lifetime, but she sounded perfectly composed and cheerful, if a little surprised to have heard from her daughter at that time of day. 'No, the girls are fine,' she assured her. 'Why are you asking? They're in the dining room right now, doing one of your old jigsaws. How's your holiday, are you having a good time ...?' And so Gill had driven on to Clermont-Ferrand, shaken but thankful. And had tried to explain to Stephen, that evening, why she had been so frightened, only to find herself blocked by his habitual wall of amused, indulgent scepticism. 'It seemed such an unpropitious omen,' she had said. 'So very strange ...' 'Oh, you and your omens,' Stephen had laughed, somehow managing to sound, as was his annoying way, entirely dismissive and yet not unsympathetic. And the next day they had returned home, the marital crisis unresolved and the omen unaccounted for: except that Gill had been forced to accept, on this occasion, that her anxiety had been fanciful. She allowed the incident to remain undiscussed, after that, but it left her with one more itch of dissatisfaction: a nagging awareness that she had allowed herself to fall in (as so often) with her husband's more prosaic way of thinking.

That itch had never really left her: Gill could feel it even now, years later, as she drove along the

Shropshire road which in her childhood she had travelled at least twice every month. As a family, they had always taken this route to visit her grandparents, and although the memories associated with it had long lain dormant, today it came home to her that these fields, these villages, these hedgerows, were still inscribed upon her memory; they were the very bedrock of her consciousness. She looked around her and wondered how she would attempt to describe them to a blind person; to Imogen. The sun, which had been so dazzling this morning, had long ago been hidden behind thick banks of grey cloud, bulbous with the threat of snow. The whole world was monochrome now: everything was black, white or some shade of grey. Trees black and brittle against a grey sky, like charred bones; rough stone walls fuzzy with layers of grey moss; the fields, rising and falling in gentle undulations, English and undemonstrative, and grey as the snow-heavy sky itself. And now the flakes started to fall, thick, spiralling flakes, big as autumn leaves, and Gill, shivering convulsively, realized that the cold in her car was gelid – raw as the cold in her aunt's house, or even worse – and the heater still wasn't working properly, and she suddenly found herself wondering, in a kind of fury, why it was that she still clung to this country, why it was that to tear herself away from it would feel like an amputation, when it never seemed to have nourished her, never given her what she wanted. The feeling came out of nowhere, knocked her sideways, as she cast bitter reflections over some of the conversations she'd had with Stephen recently, conversations about all the things they could do now that the girls had left, all the different countries and places they might visit or even choose as a new home. And she understood, at that moment, that those conversations had not been real; that she had been talking to herself, that what she had said to her husband had sounded, to his ears, like meaningless noise, while she babbled on like someone who is describing last night's dream over the breakfast table to a listener who is bored witless by the details of something which he can never himself experience at first hand.

*

On a Wednesday morning in February, four months after she had made that journey, Gill took a train down to London. In her suitcase was the envelope addressed to Imogen, still unclaimed and unopened. Of the five letters she had originally sent, three were never answered, and two were answered by people who turned out not to be the woman they were looking for. Advertisements had been placed, repeatedly, in every newspaper and magazine. Gill had contacted the Royal National Institute for the Blind, but they had no record of Imogen. Searches on the internet threw up tens of thousands of results, all of which turned out to be irrelevant and misleading. Gill's ideas were about to run out, and she was beginning to wonder if it might still be possible, even today, for someone to vanish without trace, into the ether. Finally she had decided (with her daughters' eager collusion) that it would now be sensible to listen to Imogen's tapes, if only in the hope that they might contain a clue to her whereabouts.

She checked into her hotel and then walked across Regent's Park towards Primrose Hill, where Catharine had recently found a small flat to rent. When she arrived, slightly shell-shocked as usual by the traffic noise and the pace at which everybody in London now seemed inclined (or compelled) to live, both sisters were waiting for her.

'Did you bring it?' Elizabeth asked, answering the door without even saying hello.

'Of course I brought it. Lovely to see you too.'

They kissed, and Elizabeth led her up four flights of stairs to the attic rooms, where all Catharine's familiar chaos was laid out. Gill looked around approvingly, still enjoying a thrill of recognition – more than that, of inexplicable relief – whenever she saw these books again, these pot plants, the scattered clothes and magazines, the music stand and flute left lying carelessly by the window, the old pine desk strewn with sheet music and scraps of manuscript paper. Taking it all in with a rapid, expert glance, she also scanned the flat for signs of Daniel, the boyfriend she instinctively mistrusted, for no reason that she could explain to herself or anyone else. Although she could hardly stop Catharine from seeing him, she was firmly against the idea (which had more than once been mooted) of him moving into this flat. But there were no stray underpants or electric razors or textbooks on literary theory; none that she could see, anyway.

'Hi, Mum,' said Catharine, coming over from the sink in the corner, with soapy hands. 'Did you bring it?'

'Is that the only thing you two can think about?' Gill reached into her bag and took out the manila envelope. 'It's here, OK?' She laid it on the coffee table, and both her daughters leaned over to inspect it, as if they suspected their mother of trying to deceive them. 'A cup of tea would be nice,' she added.

While Elizabeth attended to this, Gill asked her elder daughter: 'Are you nervous about tonight?'

'Not really,' said Catharine. 'I don't get nervous any more. Besides, it's only in front of friends.'

But Gill didn't quite believe her.

*

The afternoon light soon faded. It took Catharine a long time to prepare what seemed to be quite a simple lunch, and at three o'clock they were still sitting amidst its debris, beneath the muted, greenish glow cast by an overhead lamp. Gill, who did not normally drink wine at this time of day, felt her perceptions beginning to dull, and found herself staring intently, for no reason, at the gleaming bell of her wine glass, mesmerized by the peculiar paleness of the golden liquid as she swirled it gently in her palm. Outside, an ochre sun would soon be washing its last tired light over the North London rooftops, and the sky would purple into darkness: the topmost branches of the plane tree in the front garden pattered feverishly against the windowpane. Another kind of light began to glint: the flash of Elizabeth's blade as she deftly peeled and quartered an apple. She wordlessly passed the pieces around. It was some minutes since anybody had spoken. London seemed quiet this afternoon: even the inevitable police sirens were distant, unaffecting, like rumours of war from a country you knew you would never visit. Finally Gill rose to her feet and fetched the manila envelope from the other side of the room. She placed it on the table between them without ceremony.

'What time will we have to leave, do you think?' she asked Catharine.

'The concert starts at eight. So I suppose seven o'clock, to be on the safe side.'

'Right. We'd better get on with it, then.'

Gill took the fruit knife, wiped it on a paper napkin, and slit the envelope open. Then she took out the four tapes and stacked them on the table, neatly, in numerical order.

'Four C-90s,' said Elizabeth, thinking aloud. 'If each of these are full, that means six hours altogether. We won't have time to listen to them all now.'

'I know,' said Catharine. 'But at least let's get started.' She stood up and added: 'I'll make some more coffee.'

Gill took the first tape from the top of the pile and squatted down beside Catharine's stereo system. She hesitated, bewildered by the minimalist chic of the fascia, until Elizabeth crouched beside her, took the tape from her confused fingers and quickly set it up to play.

Gill and Catharine sat side by side on the low, saggy old sofa. Elizabeth sat opposite them, on a red hi-back swivel chair that Catharine had picked up cheap from an office sale a few months ago. They clutched their mugs of coffee, feeling the heat of the liquid transmit itself into their chilled and stony fingers. Catharine picked up the remote control, turned the volume up loud, and the first thing that they heard, after a few seconds, was a surge of hiss, followed by the boom and crackle of a microphone being turned on and then adjusted, scraped along a hard surface upon its plastic stand. Then there was a cough, and a clearing of the throat; and then a voice, the voice they had all been expecting to hear, although that did not make it any the less ghostly. It was the voice of Rosamond, alone in the sitting room of her bungalow in Shropshire, speaking into the microphone just a few days before she died.

The voice said:

I hope, Imogen, that you are the person listening to these words. I'm afraid that I cannot regard that as a certainty, because you seem to have disappeared. But I am trusting to fate – and more importantly, to the ingenuity of my niece Gill – to ensure that these recordings find their way to you, eventually.

Perhaps I should say no more on this subject ... but it has worried me, in recent years, that you have not reappeared in my life. I am half-inclined to read something morbid into it, but no doubt I am more prone to such thoughts at this particular moment, when my own end is so – well, so palpably close. I'm sure there is a logical explanation. Various logical explanations, for that matter. Most likely, when your family – your *new* family, that is (I cannot think of them as 'your' family, even after all this time, which is probably foolish of me) – when they decided, more than twenty years ago, that you were not to have any contact with us any more – with *me* any more, to be more specific, since I was the only one maintaining contact with you at that stage – then they would have been in a good position to make a thorough job of it. You were very young. There was your disability. (Are we still allowed to use that word, nowadays?) Easy enough, I would have thought, to cut all the ties and burn all the bridges. So perhaps that was what they did. Destroyed all the letters and other documents, threw out all the photographs. Anything like that would have posed a threat to them. You may never have been able to *see* those photographs, after all, but there was always the chance, wasn't there, that one day somebody might try to describe them to you?

And that brings us, Imogen, very much to the business in hand. The reason why I am speaking to you now. I am reaching the end of my life and for reasons which will, I hope, become apparent to you as you listen to this recording, I feel an obligation towards you, a sense of duty which has not yet been fully discharged. There are different ways in which I could relieve myself of this feeling. Of course, I am going to leave you some money. That goes without saying. But there are other things which are not so easily done. There is something else which I owe to you; something far more precious; something which is, I suppose, in the most literal sense of the word, priceless. What I want you to have, Imogen, above all, is a sense of your own history; a sense of where you come from, and of the forces that made you.

It seems to me that without such a sense you are at a great disadvantage. And that this in itself is compounded by your other disadvantages. One of the ways in which most people, most young people, acquire this sense of themselves is through looking at photographs: photographs of themselves, when they were children, and photographs of their parents and grandparents and even older relatives. But you have never been able to do this.

I say 'never'. Perhaps there was a time, before you lost your sight, when your mother showed you one or two such things. But you would have been only a very small girl – three years old – and I very much doubt whether they could have made any impression, on such a young and undeveloped mind. Since then, there would have been nothing. Which is why I'm going to do the best I can, if it isn't already too late, to correct the situation.

There are hundreds of photographs I could have chosen, Imogen. Hundreds and hundreds, going right back to the war and beyond. A few years ago, after my friend Ruth died, I sorted through them and threw away the ones that I didn't want to keep. And in the last few days, I have been looking through those that I kept, and trying to decide which ones I should now set aside and attempt to describe to you. In the end, I have settled on twenty. Twenty seems a manageable number, somehow. Twenty scenes from my own life, mainly, because I suppose that is what I am also proposing to tell you: the story of my own life – up to the point where you left it, so soon after making your first appearance. I hope that it won't seem entirely irrelevant to you. Doubtless I shall digress, sometimes, but everything I shall tell you is connected, in my mind at least, and if I can't get you to understand that, then I shall have failed.

As much as possible, however, I shall just try to describe whatever I see in the photographs. I want you to know what they looked like, the people who came before you; the houses that they lived in, the places they visited. If you can know these things, if you can somehow imagine them inside your head, then that will give you ... well, it will give you *something*, I hope. It will give you a context, in which to understand the difficult things, the painful things you will hear at the end.

Because there is a story that you don't know, Imogen. A story about your family, and me, and most important of all, about yourself. Perhaps your – perhaps the people who brought you up, have told you some of it. Some distortion of it, most likely. But they cannot know the truth, because only I know that.

Soon now, I hope that you will know it too.

Very well. I'm going to start, now. Picture number one: a suburban house in Hall Green, a few miles from the centre of Birmingham.

I was six years old when war broke out. My sister, Sylvia, was fifteen. It's always been a mystery why my parents waited nine years to have another child. This has never been explained to me. But then family life is full of mystery.

This is rather a tiny picture. I'm not sure how much I'm going to be able to describe to you. Taken in winter, and the winter of 1938 or '39, I would have thought. It shows the whole of the front of the house. The drive is on the left: it rises steeply from the road to the side gate and is very short, just about long enough to hold a car. Not that we had one, in those days. My father would cycle to work, and Mother would walk or take the tram.

Let me concentrate. A thin layer of snow covers almost everything. There is a little wrought-iron gate at the side of the house, but you cannot see down the passageway into the yard which I remember lay

35

beyond it. My father used to keep his bicycle in that passageway, it may be that you can see the handlebars peeking out in this picture, but I may be imagining it. That part is very shadowy.

To the far left of the picture, slightly overhanging the wrought-iron gate, you can see a few withered branches. These belong to my father's apple tree. It almost never bore any fruit: I don't suppose this year was any exception. But it was good for climbing, I remember. Later on, when we moved, we had four or five apple trees in the back garden. But there was no back garden at this house. Just this one patch of earth where my poor old father tried his hardest to grow some fruit for us.

These houses were semi-detached, and I suppose built at the end of the last century. The nineteenth century, I mean. Small, unyielding, redbricked houses. You couldn't enjoy much of a life in them. Looking at this picture, I can make out the number, forty-seven, just above the letterbox in the front door, which my father painted yellow, I remember. There are no colours here, of course; it is a black-and-white photograph. Next to the door is a small frosted window, with a design on it, in stained glass. I can remember this design very clearly. A circle of red – deep, ruby red – with spokes of green and lemon-yellow radiating from it. Little green triangles at each of the four corners. I can remember sitting at the foot of the stairs in the hallway and looking at this window, watching the way the sunlight would brighten and darken behind it, with the passing of the clouds. The play of colours, like a kaleidoscope. This is one of my earliest memories, I think. Perhaps I did it many times, perhaps just the once. As I try to remember it, I can hear the sweep of my mother's broom near by, behind me, on the lino in the kitchen. The two things – the image and the sound – go together in my memory. These things have resonance for me – an enormous, almost supernatural resonance – but it's terribly hard to convey that, in words. To you they will probably seem banal.

Well, back to the photograph. I have just noticed something which allows me to date it a little more exactly. To the right of the drive – the drive that is just large enough to hold a car – is an area of grass, of about the same size, with a little sumac tree in the middle. This was what we used to call – rather laughably – the 'front garden', and it did not shelve as steeply as the drive, so that near the bottom, just by the pavement, there was quite a sharp drop from the one to the other. After my friend Gracie fell over this drop and hurt herself, my father put up a little wooden fence; and you can see it in this picture, see the snow which forms an even carapace along the topmost beam. The snow looks clean and white and fluffy enough to eat: which is just what I would do sometimes, creaming it off with a sweep of my gloved hand and then taking an icy, tingling bite out of it, feeling it crumble and melt on my tongue. There's nothing like the taste of freshly fallen snow. Anyway, my father took down that fence not long after the war broke out and used it for firewood; but I am sure it was still there when Gracie was evacuated, because I can remember leaning on it that morning, and watching her go by. That was in the autumn of 1939. So the picture was taken before that. The winter of 1938, in all probability.

Do you know, Imogen, about the evacuation of children during the Second World War? (I've no idea what they taught you, in those schools of yours. I know that ignorance is rife among children today. But then, you're not a child! I keep forgetting that, have to go on reminding myself. In my mind, you are frozen, still the age at which I last saw you, when you were seven years old.) The biggest upheaval came at the very beginning of the war, when hundreds of thousands of children – more than a million, even – were taken away from their parents by train in the space of a few days. I did not experience that phase, myself. That turned out to be something of a false alarm, and most of those children were back with their families not long after Christmas. And then, in the late summer of 1940, when the Blitz started, the process began again, although less systematically than before. This time my father knew that the threat was real, and something had to be done. But I was one of the lucky ones, having family in the country. The people who took me in were not strangers, absolutely. Whereas poor Gracie was not so fortunate.

A photograph is a poor thing, really. It can only

capture one moment, out of millions of moments, in the life of a person, or the life of a house. As for these photographs I have in front of me now, the ones I intend to describe to you . . . they are of value, I think, only insofar as they corroborate my failing memory. They are the proof that the things I remember – some of the things I remember – really happened, and are not phantom memories, or fantasies, imaginings. But what of the memories for which there are no pictures, no corroboration, no proof? I'm thinking, for instance, of that day not long afterwards, the day the evacuees walked past, the day that Gracie left. Our house was on the route between the school and the railway station, so we were able to watch the whole sorry procession. They came early in the morning, at about nine o'clock, I suppose. How many children? Perhaps fifty (although I'm merely guessing), led by their teachers. None of the children were wearing school uniform, and all they were carrying were their gas masks in one hand, and little suitcases or knapsacks in the other. They also had labels tied around their necks. Gracie was near the front of the procession, walking side by side with another friend of hers, a boy of whom I was wildly jealous, someone she often chose over me in the school playground. I've forgotten his name now. They were laughing and playing a silly game together, seeing who could walk backwards for the longest, or something like that. I felt a terrible pang of envy but at the same time I couldn't understand why they were looking so happy, because my mother and father had told me what evacuation was all about, and for some reason – even though I was no older than Gracie – the meaning of it had sunk in, and I knew that something terrible was happening, that she really was going to be leaving home that day and nobody knew when she would be coming back. My mother was standing next to me, perhaps with her hand on my shoulder, and then something happened, something to do with the fence, which is really why I remember all of this so well. Where I was standing, the fence had a hole in it, a little knothole, and I was exploring this hole with my finger as the children walked by. And then suddenly I realized that my finger was stuck. A panic took hold of me and for the next few seconds (it can't have been longer than that, although of course it seemed an eternity) all I could think of was the horrible prospect that I might be there for ever, that I would never be able to pull my finger free. I pulled at my finger desperately and forgot to look at the children walking by, until my mother shook me by the shoulder to draw my attention to the fact that Gracie was waving at me, and then at last I raised my left arm – my free arm – to wave to her, but of course it was too late, Gracie had gone by, and was not looking at me any more. I didn't wonder then, but I wonder now whether she was hurt by the way I ignored her, whether she felt rejected because I didn't wave to her at the beginning of this great adventure. Certainly, when I saw her again – three or four years later, it would have been – she treated me differently. But there may have been other reasons for that.

What was waiting for Gracie at the other end of her train journey? I can only imagine. I seem to remember her telling me that she was taken to somewhere in Wales. I can picture a big, draughty room – a church hall, perhaps – and a crowd of children huddled together in the centre, tired after their long train journey, frightened now, the morning's excitement having long since worn off. They would probably have been asked to line up, and then the grown-ups would have stepped forward, strange, severe-looking women who would have scrutinized the children's faces and clothes before picking them out one by one, like customers at a Roman slave market. No words would have been spoken. But slowly the crowd of children would have got smaller and smaller, and Gracie would have seen all of her friends disappear, whisked away through the door to the unknown, darkening world outside, even the little boy who made me so jealous and whose name I can't remember, until she was one of the few left, and then it would have been her turn, at which point an exceptionally forbidding face would have loomed over her, made no less forbidding by its unnatural attempt at a smile, and she would have felt herself gripped by the wrist and led away, out into the unfamiliar dusk.

The last thing I can imagine is Gracie standing in a hallway. The hallway is dark and she has put her suitcase down beside her. The woman has gone upstairs somewhere, on some mysterious errand, and she is left alone. She thinks of this morning, already a fickle, distant memory: how she tried to wave at me, and I never waved back. She thinks back further than that, to the moment when she said goodbye to her parents: her mother's last, stifling, frantic embrace. She realizes now, with a terrible certainty, that she is not going to see her mother again tonight. She does not realize, yet, that she won't be seeing either of her parents for weeks, months: a lifetime, in a child's mind. But even the thought of one night's separation is enough to make her start crying. She looks up at the sound of footsteps descending the stairs and hopes that this strange, silent woman is going to comfort her and be kind.

Of course, I've no idea if it was like that at all. All I know is that Gracie had changed, when I saw her again, towards the end of the war. She told me nothing about her time away from home. As I say, she treated me differently. We never became play-mates again. And she spoke, by then, with a terrible stammer. I wonder if she ever lost it.

Number two: a picnic.

A family group. Aunt Ivy, and Uncle Owen, in the background. In the foreground, three children – including me. But I will come to the children later. Let me tell you about Ivy and Owen first of all.

I don't remember this picnic, and I can't identify the landscape in which the picture was taken. But it is recognizably Shropshire – I can *feel* that, just by looking at it. And probably not far from Warden Farm, the house in which they – we – were all living at the time. I certainly don't remember being taken on many excursions far afield, during those months. Most likely this was taken somewhere near the edge of the grounds, and the fields in the background belonged to Owen himself. It was taken in late autumn or winter because there are no leaves on the trees: they stand out black and skeletal against a sky which time has bleached white. I don't know why we were having a picnic at this time of year: everybody in the photograph looks cold. I suspect it was one of those sunny but bitterly cold autumn days, because Ivy is wearing sunglasses and yet her hair is being blown out of shape by the wind.

What can I remember about her, from looking at her face in this photograph?

Ivy, you should know first of all, was my mother's sister. There was not much family resemblance, however. She is smiling here, a good open-mouthed smile: everybody is doing this, in fact, so I would imagine that the picture was taken by Raymond, her elder son, and that he must have been clowning around while he was taking it. Even I seem to be smiling, a little bit. But what Ivy's smile makes me think of is her laugh: a real smoker's laugh, rough and throaty. And as soon as I think of her laugh, as if by some process of sensory association, I find myself remembering her smell. Strange how so few of our strongest memories are visual: it's something I would like to talk to you about, Imogen – one of the many things. Because your memories, I'm sure, are just as strong as mine, just as strong as the memories of any of us who are 'sighted', as I believe it's called – perhaps even stronger.

Anyway – Ivy's smell, I believe I was talking about. This is not to say that she was in any way malodorous, nothing like that. It was a strong smell but in many ways an appealing one. I think it was a mixture of whatever perfume she used to wear, and dogs. There were always at least five or six dogs at Warden Farm. Spaniels, mainly. Was I aware of that, before I was sent there? I think I was, I think it was one of the things my father said to me in order to make me feel better about it. 'They have lots of dogs,' he would have said. 'You love dogs.' Which is true. I've always loved dogs, although I've never kept one myself. And I adored all the dogs at that farm, and the way the house always seemed to smell of dogs, and the way that Ivy did, as well. It was certainly one of the things I liked about her. Children are rarely fastidious about such matters. They want to feel comfortable around a person, more than anything else.

Uncle Owen drove a green Austin Ruby, in those days. For some reason, my mother and father did not take me to the farmhouse themselves: he came to collect me. It was a Sunday afternoon. He was alone, and I can remember sitting in the front seat, barely tall enough to see out through the windows. A ride in a car, any car, was uncommon. I had certainly never sat in the front of a car before. The reason I am mentioning this now is that this car, too, smelled of dogs. It was a comforting smell. I did not like Uncle Owen. He was a man who made no effort to communicate with children or put them at their ease. He was a great grunter, but not much of a talker. I am confident that he barely said a word to me during that journey. I am thinking that it was late in the afternoon, and as we drove out of Birmingham and past the outskirts of Wolverhampton and into the countryside, the sun was setting and sending splinters of sad, low orange-red light across the treetops and hedgerows. But I think this is something I am now imagining, not a memory at all.

The more I look at Ivy's face in this photograph, the more it serves to remind me, not of what she used to look like, but of her smell, and the sound of her voice. And when I think of how she greeted me when our car pulled into the farmyard that Sunday afternoon, this is how I remember her: the warm, gravelly voice, stretching out the word 'Hallo' to five times its normal length, so that hearing it felt like being pulled out of cold water and having a thick blanket thrown around you; and then her arms enfolding me, swaddling me with that lovely smoky canine scent. That was how she greeted me on the back doorstep and if she had always been that way, for all the time I ended up staying there, then everything might have turned out quite differently.

However, there is no value in such reflections.

Ivy's hair was reddish. Strawberry blonde might be a better way of putting it. She wasn't a delicate woman, by any means. In this picture, for instance, her sunglasses are sitting snugly on a nose which is, not to put too fine a point on it, large. There were a lot of large noses on that side of the family; it also has to be said that Ivy was partial to a drink. I shall just offer you that observation, and say no more. She is wearing a rather smart jacket, nicely cut, over a long floral-patterned skirt. In fact one of the striking things about this picture is how well dressed they both look. And how formal. Uncle Owen is wearing a tie, for heaven's sake! On a picnic! But that is how things were, in the 1940s. Perhaps it is the effect of the tie, but here he looks almost handsome. He was always a big man, thick-set – it was inevitable, as he grew older, that he would run to fat – but there is no coarseness in his features. I remember him as rather a coarse man, but I think that had to do more with his manner than his looks. He has assumed a slightly strange position, crouching rather than sitting down, and this gives him a kind of tense, coiled quality, like a trap about to spring. He is gazing at the camera with enormous intensity. All I can say about this pose is that it is uncharacteristic.

So much for the adults. Now, apart from myself, the two children at the front of the photograph are Ivy and Owen's younger son, Digby, and their daughter, Beatrix. They were my first cousins, of course. I should also mention something else about Beatrix, in case you are not aware of it: she was your grandmother.

When this photograph was taken, she would have been eleven. She is sitting upright, almost as though she has just sat on something uncomfortable. Her back is rigid. Bea's posture was always good: she always carried herself well. She is wearing a cardigan, which, if my memory serves me correctly, was pale green. From the way it hangs on her body, you can see that her breasts are just starting to develop. Her hair is black, and quite short, but windswept: two strands hang over her eyes, one of them falling almost down to her mouth. Quite a fashionable cut, even by today's standards, I would have thought. Her smile is broader than anyone else's. Funnily enough, I never think of her smiling, but, looking through all of these photographs, I realize that she smiled all the time; when she was young, anyway. And it was like her mother's smile, too – never far from an out-and-out laugh. Perhaps it is because many of the older photographs I have found of her capture her in social situations. Beatrix came alive when there were a lot of other people around: with friends, at parties – any occasion when drink was flowing and the everyday cares of the world could be forgotten. Whenever she was alone with me, she was a different person: insecure, ill at ease, afraid of the world. I do not think that this is just an effect I have on people. I think that this was her true self emerging. Fundamentally I believe that she disliked herself and that to be left alone, with only her own self for company, was the very thing that she feared the most. But I realize that I am projecting, now, a lot of things that I learned about Beatrix subsequently on to her character as an eleven-year-old girl, and I must not allow myself to race forward like this.

Sitting next to her is her brother Digby. It is not important that you know very much about Digby. Like Raymond, the elder brother, he took little notice of me. This was upsetting at first, but later on, when Beatrix and I became close, it suited us quite well. He looks younger here than his thirteen years. Perhaps because he is wearing shorts. He is squatting, rather than sitting, and his calf muscles seem extremely well developed, I must say. He was a vigorous, athletic boy. There was a tennis court in the far reaches of the grounds and he and Raymond would often play there. They were both good players. They led charmed, perhaps spoiled lives. The war barely touched them. Living on a farm meant that the family was not affected by rationing; in fact they made a good profit, selling their surplus on the black market. The closest they ever came to the fighting was when a German bomber shed its load at random on a flight back from Wales and blasted a crater in one of the corn fields, about a mile from the farm. That happened while I was there. I can remember hearing the explosion, being woken up in the middle of the night and running to the bedroom window along with Beatrix. We could see the fire burning through the trees, and the next morning we were allowed to go with the boys to look at the crater. I am wandering from the point again . . .

The only person left to describe, now, is myself. My eight-year-old self. No need to look too closely at what I'm wearing: I can remember exactly. I think I only had about three changes of clothes with me for the whole time I stayed at Warden Farm. Here I am wearing my faithful old thick brown woollen jumper, knitted for me by my mother. She was an enthusiastic – one might almost say obsessive – knitter. Sometimes she did it the usual way, by hand, but she also had a knitting *machine* – a simply gigantic, baffling contraption made up of cogs and levers and pistons which took up most of our dining table at home. (I'm surprised it never collapsed under the weight.) This was the machine she would use, for two or three hours every night, knitting woollens for the troops. 'Comforts', she called them. The brown jumper I wore was just a by-product of all this activity, but I was devoted to it. It was the same brown, almost exactly, as the rough corduroy trousers I am also wearing in this picture. The ensemble is completed by a polo-necked shirt, which was a lovely autumnal golden colour. The colour of leaves on the turn.

Shropshire itself was golden. That was the thing I noticed about it at once, when I woke up on the first morning of my evacuation and drew back the curtains. I looked out across the beautiful manicured green of the front lawn, like the green baize of the table in the billiard room, and after that all I could see were fields of blazing gold, beneath a rich blue sky. Shropshire blue, Shropshire gold. It may seem like an odd thing to say but the whole *colour* of the county had changed in the last few months. There was a reason for this. (There is a reason for everything, in case you haven't learned it yet, in your short life. In fact, the story I am trying to tell you will demonstrate as much – if I tell it properly.) The reason being, in this case, that the government had recently been telling farmers to grow as much corn as possible. 'Food is a munition of war,' they were told, 'and the farm should be treated as a munitions factory.' And so, where once there had been green, now there was gold. I looked out of the window that morning, and for a moment, a brief moment, my heart soared and the terrible knowledge that had been crushing me for the last few hours – the knowledge that I had been banished from my parents' house, sent into an undeserved and inexplicable exile – was lifted from me. I turned to share this moment with my cousin Beatrix, who slept in the attic bedroom with me, but her bed was empty and the bedclothes were dishevelled. She was always an early riser, always downstairs before me. Such was her appetite for breakfast and, more than that, for life itself.

Actually, I am allowing my imagination to run away with me again. Whether I looked across, on that first morning, and saw Bea's empty bed, I really cannot say. It happened that way many mornings. Whether that was one of them is another matter. I can see that this photograph has done its work and further memories, more general memories of those few months, are starting to come back to me. Time to move on.

Number three: the caravan.

I have not yet described Warden Farm – the house itself – in any detail, but I think I will talk about the caravan first. It was one of the first things that Beatrix showed me in the garden, and it quickly became the place where we would retreat and hide together. You could say that everything started from there.

Aunt Ivy gave me this photograph herself, I remember, at the end of my time living at her house. It was one of her few real acts of kindness. Beneath her warm and welcoming exterior, she turned out to be a rather distant, unapproachable woman. She and her husband had built for themselves an active and comfortable life, which revolved mainly around hunting and shooting and all the associated social activities which came with them. She was a busy organizer of hunt balls, tennis-club suppers and the like. Also, she doted on her two sons, athletic and sturdy boys – good-natured, too, but not very well endowed in the brains department, it seems to me in retrospect. None of these things, at any rate, made her inclined to expend much of her attention on me – the unwanted guest, the evacuee – or indeed on her daughter, Beatrix. Therein lay the seeds of the problem. Neglected and resentful, Beatrix seized upon *me* as soon as I arrived, knowing that in me she had found someone in an even more vulnerable position than her own, someone it would be easy to enlist as her devoted follower. She showed me kindness and she showed me attention: these things were enough to win my loyalty, and indeed I have never forgotten them even to this day, however selfish her motives might have been at the time.

The house was large, and full of places we might have made our own: unvisited, secret places. But in Beatrix's mind – though I did not understand this until later – it was 'their' place, it belonged to the family by whom she felt so rejected, and so she chose somewhere else, somewhere quite separate, as the place where she and I should pursue our friendship. That was why we spent so much of our time, during those early days and weeks, in the caravan.

Let me see, now. The caravan itself is half-obscured, in this picture, by overhanging trees. It had been placed, for some reason, in one of the most remote corners of the grounds, and left there for many years. This photograph captures it just as I remember it: eerie, neglected, the woodwork starting to rot and the metalwork corroding into rust. It was tiny, as this image confirms. The shape, I think, is referred to as 'teardrop': that is to say, the rear end is rounded, describing a small, elegant curve, while the front seems to have been chopped off, and is entirely flat. It's a curious shape: in effect, the caravan looks as though it is only half there. The trees hanging over its roof and trailing fingers down the walls are some kind of birch, I believe. The caravan had been placed on the outskirts of a wood: in fact the dividing line between this wood – presumably common land – and the furthest reaches of Uncle Owen's property was difficult to determine. A more modern caravan might have had a picture window at the front; this one, I see, had only two small windows, very high up, and a similar window at the side. No surprise, then, that it was always dark inside. The door was solid and dark, and made of wood, like the whole of the bottom half of the caravan – even the towbar. That's an odd feature, isn't it? – but I'm sure that I am right. It rested on four wooden legs, and always sat closer to the ground than it should have done, because both the tyres were flat. The windows were filthy, too, and the whole thing gave the appearance of having been abandoned and fallen into irreversible decay. But to a child, of course, that simply made it all the more attractive. I can only imagine that Ivy and Owen had bought it many years ago – in the 1920s, perhaps, when they were first married – and had stopped using it as soon as they had children. Inside there were only two bunks, so it would have been quite useless for family holidays.

How many weeks was it, I wonder, before Beatrix

and I set up camp there together? Or was it only a matter of days? They say that split seconds and aeons become interchangeable when you experience intense emotion, and after my arrival at Warden Farm I was soon feeling a sense of loneliness and homesickness which I find it impossible to describe. I was beside myself with unhappiness. I would sob quite openly in front of Ivy and Owen – at the supper table, for instance – but never once, to my knowledge, did they think of telephoning my parents to tell them how miserable I was. My distress was simply ignored, by them, by the two boys – by everybody, in short, apart from the cook (who was a kindly soul), and of course by Beatrix. Even she was cruel to me at first. And yet I do think that when she finally took me under her wing, it was because she felt sorry for me, not simply because I was weaker than her, and easy to manipulate. She was lonely, too, remember, and she needed a friend. Beatrix could be a selfish person, at times, there is no doubt about that: I was to see it proved again and again over the following years and decades. But at the same time she was quite capable of love. Rather more than capable of it, I should say: she was *vulnerable* to it – that would be a better word – deeply, fatally vulnerable. And certainly, I think, during my time at the farm, she came to love me. In her way.

Her way of loving me, in fact, was to try to help me. And her first attempt to help me involved our drawing up a ludicrous plan – a desperate plan – which we resolved to carry out together. We decided that we were going to escape.

During the long afternoons, the lawn stretched out, billiard green, at the front of the house. A narrow, gravelled drive cut through it, but no cars ever used this drive. Almost nobody used the front door at all: only the children – and Beatrix and I especially. It was the back door where the men came to do their business, and so it was the back door that was watched. The cook watched it, from her kitchen, and Ivy watched it, from her bedroom, and Uncle Owen watched it, from his tiny, benighted study. There could be no escape that way. Even at dusk it would be risky – and it was at dusk that we had decided to leave.

That afternoon, sitting alone beneath the low roof, the crazy angles of my bedroom, while Beatrix was downstairs, taking food from the kitchen, waiting until the cook's back was turned, I thought once more of my own mother and father, at home in Birmingham, going about their ordinary lives. My father riding to work on his bicycle, a gas mask slung over his shoulder. My mother pinning out washing on the line in the back garden, just a few yards from the entrance to the air-raid shelter. These things, I knew, had something to do with danger, with the danger I had been brought here to escape from, the danger that they lived within, now, every minute of every day. And all I could think was that it was not fair. I wanted to share in that danger. It frightened me, yes, but nowhere near as much as this absence, nowhere near as much.

That evening, we waited until the house was quiet, until Ivy and Owen had settled down to a drink after dinner, and the boys had gone upstairs to play, and then we put on our coats and pulled back the heavy latch on the front door and we slipped outside.

She was eleven years old. I was eight. I would have followed her anywhere.

There was a thick dampness in the air, somewhere between mist and rain. The rising moon was three-quarters full, but screened by clouds. There was no birdsong. Even the sheep had fallen silent. We made no noise as we stepped out on to the grass.

Still wearing our school shoes, we scurried over the spongey moistness of the front lawn. We jumped down, over the ha-ha and on to the lower level of the garden, and made for the overgrown gap in the hedge, the opening that led to the secret path; the path that led to the secret place.

She ran ahead; I followed. Her grey school mackintosh, appearing and disappearing between the leaves.

At the end of the path was a clearing, tangled and overgrown with hanging branches and trailing ivy, and within this clearing was the caravan. The cold gripped you the moment you opened the door and stepped inside. The net curtains hung grey and filthy over the windows, ragged with moth holes, blackened with the corpses of flies. There was a small table which folded out from the wall, and two bench seats on either side of it. Nowhere else to sit down. A kettle on the stove, but the gas cylinder was long since empty. From the farmhouse, Beatrix had carried with her a brown bottle, a cork wedged loosely at the top, filled to the brim with cloudy lemonade, and over the last few days, she had been hiding further provisions here. A half-loaf of bread, solid as masonry. A wedge of cheese, Shropshire blue, crusty at the edges. Two apples from the orchard. And three biscuits, shortbread, baked by the cook, and filched from the biscuit tin in the larder at the risk of God knows what dreadful punishment.

'Let's eat some of this now,' she said; and we set to it, quietly and with great deliberation. I had not been able to eat much dinner and was hungry now even though my stomach was so tightened with fearful anticipation that I could barely force the food down.

There were a few items of cutlery still in one of the drawers, and Beatrix used a fruit knife to cut the bread and the cheese. When we had finished eating, without saying another word, she took my hand, turned it palm upward, and drew the blade of the knife along my tiny forefinger. I cried out, and hot salt tears sprang up in my eyes. But she took no notice. Calmly, she did the same to herself and then pressed her finger against mine, so that the two pools of blood mingled and coalesced.

'There,' she said. 'We're sisters now. Together. Whatever happens. Agreed?'

I nodded, still without saying a word. What I felt –

the thing that robbed me of my voice – was either terror, or love. Or both. Probably both, I think.

'Come on,' she said. 'We've got a long way to go tonight.'

We had already packed our clothes and brought them to the caravan the day before. Mine were squashed tightly into the small dun-coloured suitcase my mother herself had first packed a few weeks ago. It was not a practical arrangement, for an escape across countryside. My little knitted woollen toy, a black dog called Shadow, would not fit into the case. I was going to have to carry him. When I picked him up he gazed at me inscrutably, without expression. He was the thing I loved fourth best in the whole world, after my mother, and my father, and now Beatrix.

The light died quickly that night. When we left the caravan and closed the door behind us, the darkness was already absolute. We turned our faces away from the farmhouse and set off into the woods, leaving it behind for ever. Beatrix held my hand. The only sounds were the sounds of our footsteps, the clumsy snapping of twigs.

I know now – at least I think I know, insofar as one can ever know these things – that it was never her intention to take me home. She was old enough to know that two little girls could never walk all the way to my parents' house. But I did not know that, and I trusted her. And besides, we were blood-sisters now.

We came out of the woods and crossed the last of

Uncle Owen's fields. After that we walked for perhaps no more than an hour, but to me it seemed a hundred lifetimes. Beatrix knew that country well and she chose her route with cunning, describing an almost perfect circle. When we reached the glade where I begged her to rest, we must have been almost back at the farmhouse, but for all I knew, we could have been anywhere.

We lay down, and I clutched Shadow to my chest. The clouds had parted and the moon bathed everything in a quicksilver light. I could not stop shivering. Now I was more tired than scared, and gripped with a clinging despair, but still, there was a kind of beauty all around us. I was aware of that, even then. Beatrix put her arm behind my neck, and I pressed myself tightly against her, and we lay like that, on our backs, staring up at the stars.

'Do you think we'll get there?' I asked. 'Do you think we'll get there tonight?' And when she didn't answer, I framed another question, the one that had been puzzling me the most: 'Why do *you* want to come? Why do you want to leave home?'

'I don't like my mother and father,' she answered, after a long time. 'I don't think they love me.'

'Are they cruel to you?' I asked.

Again, she didn't answer.

In spite of myself, I began to grow sleepy. A barn owl was hooting, crying out in the night, very close to us. The trees rustled, the undergrowth was restless with hints of subtle, mysterious life. I could feel the warmth of Beatrix's body, the pulsing of blood through the arm at the back of my head. Her sensations became mine. The moon continued to rise, and with a flurry the owl launched into sudden flight, skimming away beneath the branches of the trees. The dampness had left the air. The goal I had fixed upon – reaching the city, knocking on the door of my astonished parents' house – receded and vanished. Despite the cold, I was happy here.

When I awoke, Beatrix was no longer with me. I sat up and looked around me, my heart pounding.

I could see her standing at the edge of the glade, looking out over the moonlit field. Her fragile silhouette. And I could hear voices. Human voices, although they sounded as desolate and unearthly as the low wail of the barn owl. Human voices, calling our names: her name, and mine.

Figures – a whole row of tiny black figures – appeared in the distance, coming towards us across the field. In defiance of the blackout, some of them were carrying torches, and these needles of bobbing light danced like sad fireflies as they made their inevitable progress towards Beatrix, who stood and watched, impassive, trembling slightly, but only with the cold, never thinking to turn and run, as I wanted to. And why should she? She had provoked this moment. She had intended it.

They were coming to find us.

Picture number four: Warden Farm itself.

I am guessing – from the colours, and the quality of the image – that this photograph was taken some time in the 1950s, more than a decade after the events I'm talking about. But the house did not change, in the intervening years.

It's a good picture, one which captures the house just as I remember it: handsome, solid, impressive. There are three storeys, in red brick, although most of the brickwork, on the first two storeys, can barely be glimpsed beneath the thick tendrils of ivy coiled and tangled around the sash windows. The house was built in the 1830s, and in style, as this picture shows, it was symmetrical and rather plain. On the ground floor you have a mock-Grecian portico flanked by two arched windows of the same height; above that, on the first floor, are three rectangular sash windows, and above them, on the second floor, three smaller, square windows. That's the main body of the building. Then, on either side, continuing the symmetry, two further rooms were added at ground-floor level, some time later. Both, again, have large arched and latticed windows, surrounded by dense, dark green ivy. This green is slightly darker than the green of the lawn, but not as dark as the shadows cast upon the lawn by the ancient and massive oak tree which grew at the front of the house. The branches of this tree overhang the front of the picture – the photographer must have been standing underneath the tree itself – and obscure the windows on the top floor of the house.

Two of these top-floor windows belonged to the playroom. It was a wide, low-ceilinged attic room, equipped with dolls and tin soldiers and board games which even then were in a state of some decrepitude. There was a ping-pong table, too, and an elaborate train set, laid out on a table top amidst a papier mâché landscape upon which someone, at some time, must have lavished a fair amount of energy. All of these things held a certain fascination. But no attempt had ever been made to make the room welcoming. There were no bookshelves, and the wallpaper was faded and peeling, and no fire ever seemed to be burning in the grate. For this reason, it was rarely visited. The boys never came up here, and Beatrix and I only seldom. Our domain was next door, in the crooked, oddly shaped bedroom, tucked among the eaves. Aunt Ivy and Uncle Owen slept on the first floor: so did their two sons. Their rooms were airy, regular, full of a sense of space. Ours was gloomy and enigmatic. The roof sloped at wild, erratic angles and my own bed was wedged into a tiny alcove that made it invisible from most parts of the room. I was completely screened off from the window, from the warmth of the morning sun and, at night, from the moonlight in which Beatrix would bathe as she drifted in and out of sleep. Mine was a realm of ever deeper and darker shadows.

You would think that I would have a clear recollection of what happened in the wake of our escape attempt, but I don't. It is my suspicion, now, that Ivy and Owen did not even tell my parents about it. Certainly, many years later, when I mentioned to my mother the night that Beatrix and I had attempted to run away from Warden Farm and walk all the way to Birmingham, she said it was the first she had heard of it. Were we even punished, in any way? I stayed at the farmhouse for another six months, at least, and in that time I don't remember any of the repercussions one might have expected: no being locked in our bedroom, or having to live on bread and dripping for a week; nothing worse, in fact, than a mild dressing-down from Aunt Ivy the next morning, couched not so much in terms of reproof as tremulous concern for our own safety and happiness.

And yet she did not forget the incident, or indeed forgive it. Of course, the whole village must have talked about it, for some time afterwards, and that must have embarrassed her. But I think that Ivy and Owen were enraged, more than that, by the sheer *inconvenience* to which we had put them that night.

Beatrix's duty, you see, was to remain invisible, as was mine, for that matter, once I had arrived at the house. Ivy's world revolved around herself, around her position in the village, around her social life, her bridge and tennis, and also, more than any of these, around her beloved sons and dogs. Beatrix did not show up on her radar. That is what Beatrix must have meant, I think, when she told me that her mother was 'cruel to her'. Ivy's was the cruelty of indifference.

Perhaps that makes what your grandmother went through as a child seem rather trivial. Certainly there are children, all over the world, who experience much, much worse things at the hands of their parents: naturally, I am aware of that. Even so, it seems to me important – crucially important – that one should never underestimate what it must feel like to know that you are not wanted by your mother. By your mother, of all people – the very person who brought you into existence! Such knowledge eats away at your sense of self-worth, and destroys the very foundations of your being. It is very hard to be a whole person, after that.

Only occasionally did it appear to me that Ivy was not just indifferent towards Beatrix but actually hated her. There is one incident, in particular, that stays in my mind. It was only a small thing, but it has stayed with me, over the years. It concerned a dog called Bonaparte. The family had many dogs, as I have said. There were three full-grown ones while I was there, three over-affectionate Springer spaniels. I soon came to love them, especially a Welsh Springer called Ambrose, who was also Beatrix's favourite. He had great intelligence, and great loyalty – you can't ask for much more than that, in an animal or even a human being. But Ivy for some reason was far more interested in Bonaparte. He was a black, wire-haired toy poodle, one of the most unattractive breeds. He was very stupid, and unreliable, but full of energy – I suppose that could be said of him at least. If Ivy herself was not present, he could be guaranteed to scamper around in a kind of directionless frenzy, always chasing imaginary objects, in a perpetual state of neurotic excitement. It was exhausting trying to keep him on a lead. But indoors, with Ivy for company, he only ever wanted to sit at her feet or, preferably, on her lap. He would lie there for hours, staring up at her with the glaze of unconditional love in his little round eyes. Ivy would stroke his hair and feed him little favours from her box of Cadbury's chocolates (of which she seemed to have an inexhaustible supply, even during wartime).

Now Beatrix, by and large, kept well away from this animal. It was not that she wanted nothing to do with him, but that he wanted nothing to do with her. She would have liked nothing more than to pet him, I imagine, if only because it would have made her feel closer to her mother and might have won her approval. But Bonaparte, perhaps in imitation of his beloved mistress, treated Beatrix with utter disdain. The only exceptions to this rule were at meal times, when he would occasionally deign to interest himself in some little titbit that she might offer him from her plate. The incident that I am thinking of took place, I believe, in the spring of 1942, towards the end of my stay at Warden Farm. The whole family was having dinner in the kitchen. The cook had roasted two large chickens, and Beatrix broke off a piece of one wing and tossed it to Bonaparte, who as usual was crouched beneath the table, his tongue hanging out greedily. Well, after chewing on the wing for a few seconds, he began to make the most horrific noises: a kind of anguished cough, from somewhere deep in his body, accompanied at the same time by a fearsome whine. It was obvious that a small bone had become lodged in his throat and he was choking. For a few seconds everyone just stared at him in horror. Then Aunt Ivy began to wail, her voice rising to a scream, to a pitch I had never heard before and would never have believed her capable of; no words were emerging and she was not doing anything as practical as asking someone to intervene, but all the same, Beatrix leaped forward, threw herself at Bonaparte, who was squatting in the middle of the room by now, and seized him by the jaw, attempting to force his mouth open. This didn't seem to do any good at all. In fact, Bonaparte's coughing and whining became even more distressed, until Ivy recovered her power of speech and screeched at her daughter something that sounded like, 'Stop that, you fool! You're strangling him, you're strangling him!', at which point Raymond (inevitably) leaped to his feet, grabbed the wretched creature from Beatrix's arms, and did ... *something*, I don't know exactly what – something that involved an almighty slap on the back – the canine equivalent of the Heimlich manoeuvre, I suppose – so that the little bone *shot* out of the dog's mouth and landed on the other side of the kitchen floor.

The crisis had passed. Momentarily. Bonaparte was perfectly all right, of course. It was Ivy who had to be carried upstairs (I'm not exaggerating – Raymond and Owen took one end each) and was not seen afterwards for about two days, except by Beatrix. Yes, the poor girl received a maternal summons the next day. We were playing in the caravan together, at the time, and together we trooped into the house and up the stairs to Ivy's bedroom, but Beatrix went in alone, while I lurked outside, my ear at the door. What I heard was very disturbing. It was not the words that disturbed me so much – indeed, I could hardly hear any of them – but Ivy's tone of voice. She didn't raise it, not at all. If she had, it might have been less upsetting. Throughout the five minutes or so that Beatrix was inside, she spoke in a low monotone which I can only describe – trying to choose my words carefully, here, without exaggeration – as murderous. I have never forgotten the controlled, deadly edge in her voice as she practically accused Beatrix (this was what I was told afterwards) of trying to kill the adored poodle – who lay, needless to say, stretched out across her feet at the bottom of the bed all this time, panting and hot with devotion. At the end of Ivy's monologue there was a curious noise. Not so much a slap, exactly, as a sudden *whooshing* sound, followed by a kind of snap, as if a bone had been wrenched out of shape, and then a scream of distress from Beatrix. After that there was a long period of intense silence. When Beatrix finally emerged, she was nursing her wrist, and her eyes were red and her cheeks grimy with tears. We went up to the playroom together, and after a while I asked her what had happened, but she never told me. She just sat there in silence, rubbing her wrist, but to me what has always been horrible about this episode is not the thought of what Ivy might have done to her, but the way that she spoke. It was the first time I had ever heard a mother speaking to her child in a voice so icy with hate. Sadly, it was not to be the last.

The story of Bonaparte did not have a happy conclusion. In fact it had a rather odd, not to say baffling conclusion. I shall explain what I mean by that shortly. In the meantime, I realize that I have digressed from my task of describing this photograph. Let me return to it.

The little brick wall which ran the length of the lawn, at a height of about eighteen inches, dividing it into two different levels, is what is known as a ha-ha. Whoever took this photograph was standing on the lower level, adopting a deferential position towards the house, which therefore looms over the viewer, commanding respect. But because of the angle at which the picture was taken, the house's gaze is directed obliquely, away from the camera and into the distance. The viewer remains insignificant, beneath notice, and Warden Farm instead directs its attention proudly, unruffled, over the lawns and pastures which lie obediently at its feet. Although I do not remember the house being quite as *unfriendly* as it appears here, I suppose that this chimes, figuratively speaking, with what I have been telling you about Aunt Ivy and Uncle Owen and their attitude towards Beatrix and myself. Beneath the cold glaze of their indifference Beatrix and I became allies, sisters, and the bond between us was not to be severed for a long, long time. Oh, there were to be many interruptions, many periods of separation, but they made no material difference. I always knew that would be the case. For this reason, there was sadness, but no sense of finality, when the time came to say goodbye to her, on the day the telephone rang in the stone-flagged hallway, and minutes later I found myself recalled to my parents' house – as abruptly and as arbitrarily, it seemed to me, as I had first been sent away from it all those months before.

The fifth picture for you now, Imogen. A winter scene. The recreation ground at Row Heath, in Bournville, some time in the bitterly cold early months of 1945.

I find this a hard photograph to look at. It was taken by my father, with his box camera, one Sunday afternoon. The pool which stands at the centre of the park has frozen over, and dozens of people are skating on it. In the foreground, sporting thick coats and woollen hats, looking straight into the camera, stand two figures: myself, aged eleven, and Beatrix, aged fourteen. Beatrix is holding a dog lead in her left hand, and at the end of it, sitting impatiently at her feet, is Bonaparte. Both girls are smiling, broadly and happily, with no intimation of the disaster that is about to befall them.

My father could take a good photograph: this one has been composed quite carefully. There are four distinct 'layers' to the picture, if that is the correct term, and I shall try to describe them to you one by one. First of all, in the far background, beneath a white, snow-heavy sky, you have the distant outline of the pavilion. This building loomed large in my youth: it was here that dances were held – out on the terrace in the summer, if the weather was kind – and these rather terrifying but exhilarating events used to form the backbone of what little I had in the way of a social life. It was a stylish black and white building, with high arches framing its tall French windows. You can see three of them in this picture: the remainder are obscured by trees, as is the van selling mugs of hot chocolate which was permanently stationed beside the pavilion, and the small twin bandstands which stood on the lawn beneath the terrace. It's a shame those aren't in the photograph. They would have looked festive and eccentric in the snow.

In front of the pavilion, flanking it on either side, we can see two rows of grand, domineering horse chestnut trees. The four trees in each row blur together, their branches thick and tightly interlocking, so that it looks as though there are just two of them, two massive domes made up of bonelike inter-sections, which watch over the pool like bloated sentries, keeping silent guard. Normally, they would have thrown huge, equally impressive reflections on to the pool's silvery surface, but it has frozen over today, and the ice reflects nothing: it is coarse and grainy, gleaming white streaked with grey where the shadows fall, and there are thin, reedy plants pushing their way through it in occasional clumps. This is where we can see the third 'layer' of the picture – the skating figures. Some of them are caught in motion, just a blur passing in front of the camera; others are captured in moments of strange, contorted stillness: arms splayed out, struggling for balance, knees raised awkwardly in the air. One man is keeping his left hand jammed into his pocket, while with the other arm he seems to be pointing at the ice with an outstretched finger, as if he has just spotted some sinister apparition beneath its surface. Two young women are just standing together, talking on the ice, while a teenage boy looks to be on the point of crashing into them. He is wearing short trousers, somewhat surprisingly. They all look rather poignant like this, the way the photograph has reduced them to an unnatural stillness, just when they are doing something as dynamic and joyful as ice-skating – rather like those figures embalmed in the molten lava at Pompeii, caught at the moment of their last struggle before death. How morbid my thoughts seem to be growing, recently. Most of the men are wearing flat caps – this is one of the things that dates the photograph – and that peculiar style of trouser that was so popular then, where the waistband seems to come up incredibly high, halfway up their chests by the looks of it. Rather ludicrous, I suppose, to modern eyes. You can see this because not all of them have coats on, which leads me to remember that, in spite of the frozen pond, it was quite a sunny afternoon. Beatrix and I were a little overdressed, it seems. Soon after this, perhaps, was when the thaw set in. Of course the winter of 1944–1945 was famously horrible. The blackout had ended by now, I seem to remember, and was replaced by what was known as the 'dim-out' instead. However, not only was the weather foul – I remember days and days of particularly thick and filthy fog, especially at dusk, which the cloudy light from the streetlamps could barely break through – but the news from abroad was dispiriting as well. The Germans had developed a major counterattack against the American First Army, and our hopes that the war might be over before Christmas were soon dashed. Although I still did not really take in the full ramifications of these things (I was a self-absorbed girl, capable of, but not interested in, understanding the events that were unfolding around me in the wider world, and I suppose I have stayed that way ever since) something of my parents' disappointment and pessimism must have communicated itself to me. I have a distant memory of the conversation over Sunday lunch that day; or rather, not of the conversation itself, but of the mood it created, in me and in the house. Ivy and Beatrix had driven over from Shropshire that morning. This was a great treat for me, something I had been looking forward to for weeks. Beatrix and I had been writing to each other, writing every few days, but had seen each other very infrequently. I no longer have her letters, sadly, and as to whether she kept any of mine, I have no idea. Goodness knows what she must have made of them, anyway. I should imagine she found them very childish. Hers, at this time, were displaying ever more adult preoccupations:

she was starting to write about clothes, make-up, boys – things which were of no interest to me whatso-ever. (And still aren't, I have to say.) Nonetheless, I treasured these letters because *she* was writing them, and anything that interested Beatrix – even when it involved such ineffably boring topics – was somehow touched with magic and excitement. Really, I was just thrilled that she wanted to be in any kind of communication with me: she could have been copy-ing out lists of names from the telephone directory, and I would have devoured her letters with the same breathless eagerness as soon as they dropped on to our doormat. As for seeing her in person, this was a rare treat. We had not even visited Warden Farm at Christmas, this year, for some reason, but today Ivy had decided to drive over to Birmingham – quite an adventure for her – in order to see her sister (my mother), and she was going to bring Beatrix with her so that she and I could spend a few hours together. The fact that the pool at Row Heath was frozen over made the treat all the more delicious. The two of us could go ice-skating in the afternoon, after lunch.

And so Ivy and my mother stayed indoors all that afternoon, drinking tea and catching up on the family gossip, while my father took us to the recreation ground. It was a ten-minute walk from our house, the pavements glistening with ice, Bonaparte panting and straining at the leash. Ivy had not, at first, wanted him to go with us. No doubt she would have preferred to have him sprawled out on her lap all afternoon. It was only after Beatrix had implored her, at great length, that she relented. I think it was the first time that she had ever been allowed to take him out for a walk by herself.

Oh – I haven't described the front 'layer' of the picture yet, have I? That is to say, the figures of Beatrix and myself, standing in the foreground. Well, we are leaning into one another, with our arms linked. There is a noticeable difference in height: I am standing on the left-hand side of the picture and I only come up to her shoulders. My head is slightly tilted, not quite resting upon her shoulder. My attitude might almost be described as coquettish, my eyes flirting with the camera, playing up to my father, but only in the most childish and artless of ways, whereas Beatrix, gazing directly into the lens, is smiling with a directness and an earnestness that is both mature and . . . well, and a little disturbing, now that I look at it. She is *challenging* the camera, trying to force some kind of response from it. Or perhaps the challenge is directed at my father himself. Whatever her object, anyway, the difference between us – in maturity and temperament – is every bit as visible as the difference in height. And yet Beatrix was still a child: I must remember that. What happened, in the few minutes after this photograph was taken, happened to a child. To an adult, perhaps it would have seemed ludicrous, or would at least have had a ludicrous side to it. To Beatrix, it was simply a tragedy.

It can be described very quickly: everything

happened in an instant. Beatrix now decided that it was time for Bonaparte to have some proper exercise. She let the foolish dog off his lead and waited for him to start running around in meaningless circles, as he always liked to do.

This time, however, Bonaparte did something quite different. Without hesitation, he dashed off towards the perimeter of the park, in a perfectly straight line. He ran straight up the slope towards the two rows of horse chestnut trees. What on earth was going through his little doggy mind, I haven't the faintest idea. We watched him, all three of us, smiling at first, pleased to be witnesses to this release of bottled-up energy. He kicked up little flurries of snow with his paws as he ran. And then, within a few seconds, a realization dawned upon us. He was not going to stop, or turn around. He carried on running, and passed between the trees, until he was almost out of sight. Even at such a distance he looked so happy, and eager, and full of life, that it took us all longer than it should have done to realize that something was wrong. Some strange impulse was telling him to keep going at full speed. He was not chasing anything. He was not trying to escape. He was not trying to find his way back to his beloved Ivy. His thoughts – if you can use that word about a dog, particularly one as stupid as Bonaparte – were simply fixed, with absolute determination, upon the distant horizon, and he was not going to stop until he had reached it.

He had almost disappeared from view when Beatrix

leaped into action. She shrieked 'Bony, Bony!' at the top of her voice and launched herself into pursuit. It seems almost comical now, as I describe it to you, but I can assure you, none of us thought it funny at the time. My father – carrying the ice skates, which were destined never to be used – ran after Beatrix, soon overtaking her, while I brought up the rear. We were all of us shouting Bonaparte's name and attracting a good deal of attention from the other people in the park. But we were far too slow: he had already reached the edge, run out across the road, disappeared through a gap in the hedge opposite and was by now tearing halfway across the playing fields which belonged to the Cadbury factory, still barking joyously. First of all we had to find the gate to these fields – which was about fifty yards away along the main road – and by the time we had got through it, the dog was nowhere to be seen.

'Where is he?' my father was saying, standing with his hands on his hips, panting heavily. 'Where the *devil* is he?' Beatrix by this stage was *howling*, a real blood-curdling howl, and soon enough this set me off as well – coupled with a scrape to my legs after falling over on that road. So my poor father had not one but two weeping children on his hands, as well as a dog that seemed to have become possessed by some demonic spirit and vanished into thin air.

Well. What else can I tell you, about that afternoon? We must have searched the surrounding streets for an hour or more, as the afternoon grew colder and darker. We called his name until our voices were hoarse. And all the time, nagging away at our minds – or my mind, at any rate – was the question, *Why?* Why had this silly little dog just run off like that, with every appearance of excitement and enthusiasm? It made no sense. It was baffling, as well as heart-breaking.

Then at last, when there was clearly no point in prolonging the search any further, there was the long, miserable return home, the breaking of the news to Ivy, and her reaction – which went through a definite sequence, beginning with silence, followed by incredulity, recrimination, shouting, hysterics and finally a sort of desperate onset of pragmatism: she and Beatrix and my father piled into Ivy's car and drove off to the nearest police station, to register Bonaparte's details. All in vain, of course. Mother and daughter were fated to drive home to Shropshire dogless, despondent and still unable to believe what had happened to them. God only knows what they talked about on the journey. I imagine that they said nothing at all. Beatrix was still crying, in any case.

I did not see her again for some time after that. There was a long interval, too, before her next letter, which contained no reference to this episode, or to Bonaparte. The dog was never found again. Once, walking through Bournville hand in hand with my mother, on the way to the dentist, I passed a man walking a dog who looked exactly like him. My mother thought so too: we both stopped and turned and stared, and the man turned and stared back, puzzled and a little indignant. But we were not brave enough to confront him.

This photograph brings it all back. And yet sometimes, the images we remember, the ones we carry inside our heads, can be more vivid than anything a camera is able to preserve on film. If I lay down this photograph, now, and close my eyes, what I see at once is not darkness but the memory of Beatrix, just before she began to run after that dog: silhouetted against the winter sky, her little vulnerable figure, black against white, standing motionless on the ridge between those two rows of chestnut trees, her back to me, looking into the distance, her gaze pitched towards the horizon, to the point where that foolish, annoying little animal was about to disappear from view. A silhouette, that's all, the outline of a human shape, and yet to me it is as expressive as if I were staring Beatrix in the face: in the tense, wired attitude of her body I can see all her despair, all her terrible sense of loss, all her horror at the thought of what awaited her when we returned to the house and told her mother the news. She had stood there, rooted, for I don't know how long – paralysed by all of these things. Just for a few seconds, I suppose, but how clearly I can still see her. The image is burned, burned on my consciousness. It has never left me, and I can be certain now that it never will.

Beatrix's wedding was a rather subdued affair, as I think this next picture illustrates.

We are up to number six, now, aren't we? And back at Warden Farm again.

A group of eight people, photographed once again in black and white, standing outside the front door. On the far left of the picture is a short, fair-haired man whose name for the life of me I can't remember: he was the best man. Then you have the groom's parents: similarly, their names are lost to me, long since lost. Then the groom himself: Roger, standing arm in arm with Beatrix. Next to her, Ivy, of course, and Uncle Owen. And last of all, to the far right of the picture – myself, the proud bridesmaid. I am fifteen years old, and the year is 1948. Late spring or early summer, if I remember correctly.

Beatrix herself was eighteen now. Far too young to marry, as I'm sure you will agree. Needless to say, she was pregnant. Why else would she have got married, at that age, to someone as obviously unsuitable as Roger?

Let me look at him more closely, so that I can describe him to you. He is not so much smiling at the camera as glowering – that is the first thing you notice. I would say, from my brief acquaintance with him, that this was his habitual expression. He was an unsmiling sort of person. Whether this reflected his general outlook on life, or merely his feelings upon finding himself married to Beatrix, and the father of her child, I would not presume to say. To be tied down to a place you do not like, at a young age, to be married to someone you don't love, and to believe that the remainder of your life will consist of efforts to provide for her and the children you do not want, would be enough to make anybody scowl, or so I would have thought. Anyway, in this picture he is scowling. His hair is cut short, and has been brushed and stiffened so that it stands upright – a bit like Stan Laurel's. His morning suit is a good cut, and a good fit – he was a well-built, athletic man: nice-looking, too, there is no denying that.

They had met a few months earlier, at a dance given in Wellington Town Hall by the Young Conservatives. Whether Beatrix herself was ever a Conservative, in any meaningful sense, is a question that I cannot really answer. She had no politics, so far as I know. Certainly, in all the thirty or more years that I knew her, I cannot recall her ever expressing a political opinion. However, she was a paid-up member of the Young Conservatives, and on the night of this dance made a considerable impression by all accounts. She was chosen as 'Miss Conservative' or some such title, and if there survived a photograph recording that occasion you can rest assured that I would have described it to you. She must have caught the attention of many young men that night, and I dare say the most handsome of them was Roger. A certain amount of beer and wine was consumed (she would not have been used to this, at such a young age), she was offered a lift home and … well, the rest you can probably imagine. Remember that Beatrix had left school a few months earlier and that she was desperate – and I do mean *desperate* – to find some way of escaping her parents' household. Whether the actual conception (your mother's conception, that is) took place that night, I cannot say with any certainty. All I know is that, three months later, she and Roger were engaged to be married. Much to the horror, I suspect, of both families. But back in those days, nobody would have had much choice in the matter.

Beatrix told me only one thing about their courtship (if that's the right word). I shall pass it on to you, if only because it suggests that, during their brief time together, it was not the case that they were at all staid or conventional, or that they never managed to have any fun. She told me that in those days Roger used to ride a motorbike – don't expect me to tell you which model, I am the wrong person to ask about that sort of thing – and they would often take rides together through the Shropshire country-side. Now, on more than one occasion, apparently, he drove her all the way up to the top of the Wrekin – which, as you must surely know, is the most visible landmark in that district: it stands at the very heart of Shropshire, and can be seen rising, bell-like, from almost every point in the county. When you climb to the summit, at a height of about one thousand feet, you find a strange rock formation with a giant cleft between two of the rocks. This cleft is known as the Needle's Eye, and it is only a few feet wide: if you are feeling really daring, you can attempt to squeeze your-self through it, which I believe can be a hazardous experience because there is quite a drop on either side. The story I remember being told, anyway, is that one evening, at sunset, Roger took Beatrix up to the Wrekin on the back of his motorbike and they actually managed to ride as far as the Needle's Eye itself. I have always found it such a romantic image! The path is very steep, very rocky, and I honestly wonder whether such a thing has ever been done again, before or since. It strikes me that any man who could take his girlfriend – or fiancée, I suppose, as she must have been then – on an excursion like that could not have been an entirely bad catch.

However. The marriage did not work out well. I suppose you have guessed that by now. I can see it all, the whole sequence of events, implied in this photo-graph, but perhaps I am being over-imaginative; and relying too much on the benefit of hindsight. Beatrix at any rate looks happy enough. She is wearing, of course, the traditional bride's outfit, all in white, despite the fact that this could not, strictly speaking, have been considered a white wedding. Her face has aged considerably since the photograph of her at the skating pond. It is noticeable how tightly she is clinging to Roger, how close together they are standing, while there must be a whole foot of distance between Beatrix and her mother. Ivy is wearing something around her neck, incidentally, which would never be countenanced nowadays. It is not so much a fur stole as an entire dead fox. You can see its beady eyes staring out at you from her left shoulder, almost as if it knew the camera was there and was determined to be as much a part of the picture as everyone else. It seems incredible now, but the wearing of such monstrosities was very much the fashion of the time. It wouldn't surprise me if Ivy had hunted the poor creature down and killed it herself only a couple of weeks before.

Ivy's face and Owen's face are masks. Both of them have just about managed to force a smile, but there is nothing convincing about them. As for me: well, I am not smiling, but I think I'm enjoying the occasion more than anybody. I was still young enough, and foolish enough, to cherish certain romantic ideals. I can remember thinking it wonderful that Beatrix should already have found someone to marry. But there is a sadness in my eyes, too, which the photographer has unwittingly caught. Beatrix and I were blood-sisters, after all. I may have had no idea what that meant, in reality, but that did not prevent me from having a primal, immovable sense that there was a special bond between us, a bond that could not be untied and could not be severed by *anybody* – least of all (though I would never have articulated this to myself) by a *man*. And so the happiness I felt for her – which was certainly far deeper and truer than anything her parents or brothers were feeling for her that day – was tempered by some shadowy, nebulous emotion that I could not have put a name to, and perhaps still couldn't: regret is too strong a word for it. So is jealousy.

It is one of those occasions where the picture, the picture itself, is far more expressive than the words I can find to describe it. You really need to see the picture, Imogen, to know what I was feeling that day. Everything is here in the picture.

Number seven. I do not feature in this one, myself. Nor in the two that follow.

However, this is a momentous photograph, for you, Imogen. It is the first appearance of your mother. Your mother, Thea!

Did you even know that that was her name? Perhaps not. They told you nothing, those people, did they?

The kitchen of the house in Much Wenlock. Roger's house, and Beatrix's. The marital home. This one is a transparency, in colour. Most of the photographs I shall be describing to you from now on will be in colour, I think. I took this myself, on my father's camera, which he must have allowed me to borrow for a few days. It's pretty obvious that I didn't really know how to use it. My object, presumably, was to preserve a record of the infant Thea, but being so in-experienced, I got the composition all wrong, so what you really have is a picture of Beatrix's kitchen, with Thea as merely one small object contained within it. As a result, it is a much more interesting photograph than it might have been. Babies are all much of a muchness, as far as I can see, but no two kitchens are the same, are they?

This one appears, first of all, to be impossibly small. I certainly remember it being narrow, but more than that, according to this picture, everything about it seemed to have been arranged in order to emphasize the impression of smallness and enclosure. The linoneum has a pattern of black and white squares, making the floor look like a chessboard. A large, heavy mahogany dresser occupies most of one wall, and the window next to it is tiny. This window looked out on to a small yard at the side of the house, and beyond that, into the garden of the house next door. To let in the light from Beatrix's own garden, you had a window in the back door, but when this photograph was taken it was covered by a chintz curtain, with a red, yellow and green floral pattern. My memory is that this curtain was kept drawn almost permanently, so that the kitchen was always in semi-darkness. Why Beatrix wanted to keep it this way, I cannot imagine. Perhaps she did not want to look at the garden, which lay infertile and untended, neglected by both Beatrix and her husband for the whole of their short tenure of that house.

The kitchen looks so cramped, in part, because it is dominated by your mother's enormous pram: an absurdly bulky and unwieldy vehicle, about the size of a small family car, it seems to me now. It has an iron frame and looks as though it must have weighed a ton

– I honestly don't know how Beatrix would ever have found the strength to push it. It is standing in the middle of the kitchen and it leaves literally no room to pass on either side. Thea is lying on her back in the pram, wrapped up in some sort of muslin blanket, her eyes shut tight with a kind of furrowed concentration, as though sleeping is yet another one of the difficult grown-up tasks she must set herself to learn. I cannot really think of much else to say about her. She has no hair to speak of, the requisite number of eyes, ears, noses and so on. Let me concentrate on something more interesting. To the right of the pram is a table which has been painted bright green. Whose idea was that, I wonder? It looks hideous. Perhaps it was that colour when they bought it. Roger and Beatrix had no money to speak of. He worked for the County Council, something to do with visiting the local farmers and checking that they were meeting production quotas laid down by the government. (In fact his work quite often took him to Warden Farm, although that was not, as I said, how he and Beatrix had met.) He picked up quite a few nice little gifts in the course of this job – not bribes, exactly, simply tokens of friendship (I'm sure this is how he would have put it) from people anxious to stay on good terms with him. What this meant, in practice, was that he and Beatrix did not have to rely entirely on their ration book, and were never short of good farm produce. There are a dozen or more brown eggs sitting in a bowl on the green table, and a big slab of yellow butter in a butter-dish. Such items were still in short supply, even then, and there would have been house-wives in Much Wenlock who would have longed to get their hands on them. What a pity that Beatrix hadn't the faintest idea how to cook. The phrase 'she couldn't boil an egg' was literally true of her. She was still just a girl, remember, and she had never been expected to do much for herself at home. Finding that she was suddenly expected to run a household must have been a terrible shock. I went to stay with them on a few occasions, and each time I was astonished by what Beatrix gave us to eat for dinner. Potatoes as hard as stones, chicken lily-white and leaking blood over the plate, runner beans that had not even been topped and tailed. Roger would push his plate aside without comment after a few mouthfuls, as if this was exactly what he had (already) come to expect, put on his coat wordlessly and go out to the pub.

It was an adventure for me, certainly, at the age of sixteen, to stay unaccompanied in the house of this newly married couple. Thinking about it, I am rather surprised that my parents were happy with the arrangement. No doubt they would have been less happy with it had they known that Roger once made a crude pass at me while Beatrix was out of the room. (Although she was only next door, in the kitchen, doing the washing up.) I was too mortified ever to mention this episode to anyone, even Beatrix herself. Roger took my rejection with perfect equanimity – indeed with that air of indifference of which he was a perfect master. He seemed blithely unconcerned – or perhaps simply unaware – that it might affect my feelings towards him, or make for an uncomfortable situation when the three of us were together. There was a matter-of-fact coarseness about him – a moral coarseness, I mean – which infected the household, and to which Beatrix herself was either indifferent or, worse still (and I do think this is the truth of the matter, in retrospect), attracted. That, above all, is why it seemed such a loveless and unwelcoming house, and why I find this picture of the darkened kitchen so evocative.

Aside from the contents of the green table, there is not much evidence of food in this photograph. The jars on the shelves of the dresser mostly appear to be empty. They look like the kind of jars in which you would keep home-made jam, but I would be amazed if Beatrix ever made any. Similarly, the way that one tin is visibly labelled 'FLOUR' and the bread-bin bears the proud inscription 'BREAD' strikes me as poignant: these are references to what they should have contained, not what was actually in them. There is a chopping board, a pair of scales with a set of weights neatly stacked beside them, a hand-operated mincer clamped to the side of the table, a large brown teapot ringed with green and creamy horizontal stripes. Everything looks cold and untouched. I wonder where Beatrix was when I took this picture. She might have been out at the shops – always a lengthy excursion in those days, the queues for the butcher's and the greengrocer's used to stretch halfway down the street – or she might just have been in the living room next door, where they kept their black Bakelite radio, tuned permanently to the Light Programme. Beatrix never listened to the news or to educational programmes or even variety shows: she only wanted to hear music, music bubbling out of the radio in a continuous stream. Light orchestral music, in the main, the sort that the BBC had started to commission from composers with the clear aim of boosting morale: jaunty, up-tempo, foot-tapping pieces which were meant to bring a smile to your face and could be fitted on to one side of a '78' record. There was one tune she was particularly fond of: the title was 'Portrait of a Flirt'. (I will not draw the obvious conclusions.) I suppose such compositions acted as a sort of musical Prozac for depressed post-war housewives. I don't know whether it worked, in Beatrix's case, but she was certainly in need of it.

The walls and door of the kitchen are painted that creamy, brownish white that was so popular at the time. It was as if people were afraid to let any real light and brightness into their lives – or it had never occurred to them that they were allowed to do so. On the left-hand side of the picture – the opposite side to the green table and the mahogany dresser – is a large and deep porcelain sink, with a blue chequered tea towel thrown over the edge to dry. Next to it is a wooden draining board, which appears to be covered with newly washed clothes, waiting to be dried – it's hard to be certain, since most of the pile is off the edge of the photograph. There is no fridge in the kitchen, I notice: not many households had them, back in those days, and in any case there is not enough room.

It's possible that I may have washed those clothes myself. It was the kind of thing Beatrix persuaded me to do whenever I visited. There was no washing machine, of course: just a basin of hot water, soap powder, a mangle and a washing line. My hands would be chapped and wrinkled for hours afterwards. I also did a fair amount of babysitting, while Beatrix went out in the evenings: by herself, that is, never with Roger. She had joined a number of local societies, throwing herself with particular gusto into amateur dramatics. She belonged, if I remember correctly, to the Much Wenlock Women's Institute Players and took a leading role in their production of *Mystery at Greenfingers*, by Priestley. As for some of her other activities – bridge clubs and sewing circles, and so on – I suspect that they were really just a pretext for bored women to get together and drink and laugh. It is very apparent to me, in restrospect, that Beatrix and Roger had no future together, from the very earliest days of their marriage. At the time, I suppose I must just have taken it for granted that this was what married life was like. I can't say that it whetted my appetite for it. But I was too young, far too young, to dream of criticizing Beatrix for accepting this. I was still devoted to her, still felt bound and obligated to her, and the only thing I felt on her behalf was sadness, really, a sort of unspoken, unexamined sadness at the thought that so much of her joy in living already seemed to have been snuffed out. I could not help seeing that she was unhappy, and desperately frustrated. It was a narrow, pinched little life they were making for themselves. Growing up where she did, Beatrix had developed a romantic and adventurous nature, and she had no outlet for it any more. The happiest times I can remember spending with them were when we drove out – twice, I think – to the Long Mynd for a picnic. Roger had long since traded in his motorbike and scraped together enough money to buy a second-hand Morris Minor. Somehow we all squeezed into this (I seem to recall sitting in the front passenger seat, Beatrix sitting behind me with the baby on her lap) and drove out for the afternoon to those wonderful Shropshire hills. I wonder if you have ever walked on them yourself, Imogen. They are part of your story, you know. So many things have changed, changed beyond recognition, in the almost sixty years since the time I'm now recalling, but the Long Mynd is not one of them. In the last few months I have been too ill to walk there, but I did manage to visit in the late spring, to offer what I already sensed would be my final farewells. Places like this are important to me – to all of us – because they exist outside the normal timespan. You can stand on the backbone of the Long Mynd and not know if you are in the 1940s, the 2000s, the tenth or eleventh century . . . It is all immaterial, all irrelevant. The gorse and the purple heather are unchanging, and so are the sheeptracks which cut through them and criss-cross them, the twisted rocky outcrops which surprise you at every turn, the warm browns of the bracken, the distant greys of the conifer plantations, tucked far away down in secretive valleys. You cannot put a price on the sense of freedom and timelessness that is granted to you there, as you stand on the high ridge beneath a flawless sky of April blue and look across at the tame beauties of the English countryside, to the east, and to the west a hint of something stranger – the beginnings of the Welsh mountains, already hinted at by one of the wilder and more eerie features of the Long Mynd itself. I mean the Stiperstones, of course, that long dark ridge of massive, serrated rocks, cast by the ravages of weather and time into weird formations, the weirdest of all being the Devil's Chair, which has spawned all sorts of fanciful and macabre legends. Anyway, now is perhaps not the time to elaborate upon those stories. I have my own story to tell, and in any case, Beatrix and Roger never took me to those more remote regions. (I first explored them a few years later, with Rebecca – but I have not yet told you who Rebecca was, and that, too, must wait its turn.) We would usually drive no further than Church Stretton, and then up to the Cardingmill Valley. There is a lovely and famous walk you can make there, up to the Light Spout waterfall and finally (although the three of us never made it that far) to the summit of the Long Mynd itself. If that landscape, to me, seemed visionary and unreal (you must remember what an impressionable sixteen-year-old I was), the response it evoked in Beatrix and Roger was – how shall I put this? – somewhat earthier. It seemed to have an almost sexual effect on them, not to mince words. I have a vivid memory of them disappearing into some shady recess, leaving me alone with Thea and the picnic things, the two of us lying side by side on the thick woollen tartan rug while her parents busied themselves secretly, their dormant animal attraction for each other reawakened, no doubt, by the sunshine and the sense you always had in this place of proximity to nature, of closeness to some primal, life-giving force. It's amazing in a way that Beatrix never got pregnant again. What kind of difference would that have made, I wonder, to subsequent events? I think on the whole it's better that it didn't happen.

I wish I had a picture of one of those picnics. I would like to look on our faces again, me and Beatrix, together, somewhere on those hills. But this picture of the kitchen, dreary though it is, tells more of the story. And it is appropriate, too, to dwell on the infant figure of Thea, your mother, as she lies in her pram, unaware of the turns her narrative is about to take, unaware that the fragile sense of security she has enjoyed in her short life up until this point is already on the verge of splintering for ever into fragments. How peaceful she looks, in her baby ignorance!

The eighth picture is quite different from those that I've chosen before. It was not taken by me, or Beatrix, or any member of our family. It was given to me, in fact, following a dinner party in London when I was well into my fifties. It features a caravan – another caravan! I am only just beginning to realize what an important part caravans play in this story. There will be other ones, too, before I am finished. But this particular caravan is rather special, and so are the two people standing in front of it. They are both actors. One of them is called Jennifer Jones, and the other is called David Farrar. I suppose it is just possible that you might have heard of them.

Where to begin? Ruth, the friend with whom I shared a good many years of my life, was a gregarious person and liked to entertain regularly. She was a painter – rather a highly regarded painter, at this time (by which I mean the late 1980s) – and the people we had to dinner were often people of similar leanings and temperament: fellow artists, writers, musicians, critics and so on. One evening we had among our guests a man who wrote what I always thought were fearsomely intellectual books about the cinema. He was not very good company, I have to say, although that is completely by the by.

The talk turned to films at one point, and our cinephile guest mentioned the director Michael Powell and his film *Gone To Earth*. He did so because he had heard that it was about to be revived at a London cinema. This was the first part of the conversation that had attracted my attention, because until then I'm afraid that it had (like most conversations about films) been boring me, and I had started to doze off. It was only when this title was brought up that I suddenly turned and addressed a question to him. 'But surely nobody remembers that film?' I said. 'I haven't heard it mentioned for years and years.' He told me that, on the contrary, the reputation of Michael Powell had been in the ascendant recently, and that this film was now regarded – by some (he stressed that word most emphatically) – as a masterpiece. 'You've seen it yourself, have you?' he asked. 'Yes,' I answered. 'I saw it in Birmingham – several times, as a matter of fact – in the winter of 1950. But never since.' 'That doesn't surprise me,' said our writer friend, and then launched into a brief *précis* of the film's disastrous fate: the producer had loathed it, apparently, and given orders for it to be reshot, re-edited, retitled and generally hacked about for its American release. In the years that followed, all traces of the original were believed to have disappeared. I was astonished to learn that it had now been restored to its former state and could soon be seen for the price of a cinema ticket and a tube journey to Oxford Street. 'But Ruth, we have to go,' I insisted, turning to her. 'We have to go and see it as soon as possible.' 'Of course, if you wish,' she answered, indifferently. 'But why is it so important? What's so special about it?' 'I would guess,' said our friend, 'that Rosamond must have seen it at an impressionable age, and it marked her for life.' To which I replied: 'Not exactly. I was at an impressionable age, yes, but not when I *saw* it. I'm talking about the time I was *in it*.'

Two days after this conversation, he sent me a photograph – a lobby card from the film, which he had retrieved from his personal collection. This is the photograph I have in front of me now. I shall describe it to you in a moment. But first of all I shall have to give you some background.

It was in a letter, written in June 1949, that Beatrix told me the astonishing news: a film crew was coming to Much Wenlock. A real film crew, making a real feature film for the cinemas, with real British and American stars. Yes – American! Because the star of the film – and this was the really unbelievable thing, for me – was going to be Jennifer Jones, who only a couple of years earlier had reduced me to a state of slack-jawed astonishment with her performance in some Western (the title will come back to me shortly) in which she played opposite Gregory Peck and flaunted a brazen, swaggering sexual energy, the like of which I had never seen or imagined before. Ah, yes, I remember now – it was called *Duel in the Sun*, and I think my parents regretted taking me to see it from the moment the credits rolled. We saw it at the old Gaumont cinema in Birmingham, and I suppose I would have been about thirteen or fourteen years old. My first real crush, it would be true to say, was on Jennifer Jones. Gregory Peck left me completely cold. Afterwards I used some of my pocket money to buy a copy of *Picturegoer* magazine which contained an article about the film. It made great play of the fact that Miss Jones (or Mrs David O. Selznick, as she had become by then) had first won fame playing a nun or some such virginal role, and yet now here she was portraying a sleazy tramp of the Old West, and the headline on the article was 'From Saint to Sinner in Under Two Years!' Funny how some things stick in the memory. Alongside the article were some pictures of Jennifer Jones in her provocative lacy costumes, her dense black hair centre-parted, bee-stung lips frozen into a pout and vixen eyes always looking slightly aslant, away from the camera. Of course I cut the pictures out and slept with them tucked furtively under my pillow, but I never told anybody about my obsession – not even Beatrix, when I wrote her one of my weekly, gushing confessional letters. I felt somehow ashamed, embarrassed by the intensity of it. And at the back of my mind, I'm sure, was the guilty suspicion that it should have been Gregory Peck I was getting excited about.

Two years later – with the pictures still in my possession, crumpled and faded, although no longer kept under my pillow – Beatrix's letter arrived, and I had to read it through many times before it made any sense to me. You have to consider my situation, Imogen: a lonely girl living in suburban Birmingham, with few close schoolfriends, practically an only child (for Sylvia, although still living with us, was now twenty-five years old and did not feel like a sister at all); it's hard to conceive of anything more remote from the world that these pictures evoked. Sensuality; glamour; the unimaginable lives lived by those godlike figures thousands of miles away in Hollywood. The idea that this world might suddenly be *within reach*, its crazy, unpredictable orbit bringing it, unbelievably, to rest for a few weeks in *Much Wenlock* of all places, was more than my childish brain could take in at first. I remember running downstairs after I had read the letter for the third or fourth time and screaming something at my mother, some hysterical, babbling attempt at conveying Beatrix's news, and being met with an incredulous dismissal: 'Oh, don't be foolish, dear' – some such words – 'Bea must have got hold of the wrong end of the stick.' But she hadn't; that was the amazing thing. It was all about to come true.

The next thing was to beg, persuade and implore my parents to let me visit Beatrix while the filming was taking place. By a great stroke of good fortune it was scheduled to start in August, during the school holidays. My mother and father had been planning to take me camping for a week, near Rhyl in North Wales, but I was already dreading it. (Can you imagine what the thought of it must have seemed like, to a sixteen-year-old girl?) Anyway, it was not difficult to dissuade them. It was agreed that I should go to stay with Beatrix and Roger instead, so I had the delicious prospect of a whole week in Much Wenlock to look forward to, while the filming was in full flow.

In the meantime I found out everything I could about the forthcoming production – which was next to nothing. I went to my local library and could find no references to it at all in the current newspapers or magazines. The best I could do was to borrow a copy of the novel upon which the film, apparently, was to be based. I devoured it in a couple of sittings and then reread it and then reread it again. I have not read it since, I must admit: my taste for that sort of overheated rustic melodrama has abated somewhat. At the time I thought it entrancing. It's the story of an ignorant country girl who marries the village chaplain but meanwhile gets caught up in a torrid affair with the local squire, while quite sensibly preferring her pet fox to either of them. At the climax she comes to a sticky end by falling down a mineshaft. I suppose that now most people would consider it silly stuff, but at the time I loved it, for being rooted in the Shropshire landscape, saturated with the colours and contours of its hills, and the author's feeling for nature is still what I remember best. There were some beautiful passages.

Anyway, all of that – like so much else – is neither

here nor there. In July there was a letter from Beatrix which contained all sorts of exciting news. Some members of the crew were already starting to arrive, including the actor who was going to play the squire. His name was David Farrar, and Beatrix didn't really know who he was, but one of her friends had seen him once in a film about nuns (another one: nuns were very popular in those days, cinematically speaking) and thought he was really 'dishy' (I believe that was the word), and then just the week before, when she – this friend – had been cycling along the road to Wellington, she had seen him coming down the same road in the opposite direction, riding a horse! She had almost fallen off her bicycle with the shock. Another thing Beatrix told me was that a notice had gone up in the market hall at Much Wenlock, saying that they needed all sorts of help with the film: they needed craftsmen and carpenters to help build the sets, and they needed good riders to be in the hunting scenes, and they needed lots of extras just to come along and be in some of the street scenes, and anyone could come and take part so long as they were able to bring their own costumes, which should be at least fifty or sixty years old. And Beatrix told me that upstairs at Warden Farm, somewhere in one of the attics, there were all these trunks and chests full of clothes that had belonged to Ivy's mother, Agatha, and she was going to go over and look through them and find some dresses that were suitable for both of us to wear, if she could.

Roger himself professed no interest in any of these doings. He gave us to understand that it was all so much female frippery, in his opinion. I thought this rather odd at first – he was not by any means immune to glamour, after all – until Beatrix informed me that her husband was already quite preoccupied, being fully absorbed in an affair with a neighbour who lived two or three doors down the road from their house. She was a very pretty half-Italian woman called Annamaria, who had annoyed Beatrix considerably a few weeks earlier by being chosen as 'Carnival Queen' of Much Wenlock, pipping her to the post by only a handful of votes. Beatrix hated her with a passion, there is no doubt about it, and she hated Roger for his betrayal, too, but she did not act as she did by way of retaliation, I don't think. What happened that summer could have been predicted from the start. It had a kind of grand inevitabilty about it.

I can describe exactly the clothes that Beatrix found for us to wear for our appearance in the film. This is not a feat of memory on my part: it's because I have the film on tape now, recorded from the television some years ago, and she and I can be seen quite clearly in one of the earliest scenes. Oh, the excitement, of glimpsing myself – just for a few seconds – on the big screen, when I saw the film with my parents when it was first released! We went and saw it four or five times in a single week, just for that thrill. (And most of the time we were almost alone in the cinema, for it was not a popular film, not popular at all.) And then the poignancy of glimpsing myself – of glimpsing *both* of us – once again, when the film was rereleased almost forty years later, and I saw it with Ruth at that cinema near Oxford Street shortly after our dinner party. *She*, I must say, was not in the least happy about this. A few years earlier (I will explain all of this in due course) she had made me promise to forget about Beatrix: not to write to her, and not to talk about her. So it was quite a concession, on Ruth's part, to come and see the film with me, but we barely spoke about it afterwards; and when it was shown on television some time later, I did not tell her that I had recorded it, and I did not watch the tape until after her death. Since then I have seen it many times – so many times; it is the only *moving* record I have of Beatrix at all, the only one where she is not frozen in time. It is precious to me for that reason, mainly, although there are other reasons too.

Our little appearance takes place in what I believe the film-makers call an establishing shot. A sculptor is seen chiselling the date – 20 June 1897 – on to a memorial stone, against a background of bright blue sky. Behind this, already, we can hear the noise of horses' hooves clip-clopping along the street. We then cut to the street itself – the bottom of the High Street, at its junction with Wilmore Street, so that the old Tudor guildhall and buttermarket buildings are also in view – and there, immediately, you can see Beatrix and me, standing in the left-hand corner of the frame, laughing and talking together. She is wearing a sailor suit with three-quarter sleeves. The blouse of the suit is Cambridge blue, but her skirts are darker, and pleated. She has a bow at her breast, and the collar of the suit is edged with white braid. On her head she wears a straw boater, I suppose to complete the nautical theme. For some reason she also has a length of skipping rope twined around her hands. I think she is meant to look like a youngish girl, although of course Beatrix was nineteen years old by now. Her hair is the same strawberry blonde as her mother's, and is tied back behind the neck. Her pale skin looks slightly pinkened; she never tanned, but always went pink, and that hot summer she had already been spending too much time out in the sun. I am also wearing a straw hat – a large, round, wide-brimmed pink hat with a single ribbon tied around it – and a red checked pinafore over a high-necked white dress. The dress's ruffle peeks out beneath the pinafore at my legs. My hair is longer than Beatrix's, much longer: it reaches almost down to my waist in two thin, wiry strands. I had forgotten that I used to wear my hair so long, in those days. I have worn it short now for more than fifty years. I am also wearing a pair of white cotton gloves, which seems a peculiar touch, for a scene which is meant to be taking place on a bright summer's day. These come into view after a few seconds, when I brush my hair back in a rather awkward gesture. (I appear to be much more self-conscious in front of the camera than Beatrix, who looks entirely at ease there.) A few yards behind us, a pony and trap crosses the screen from right to left, and a bewhiskered policeman stands directing the traffic. After the pony and trap, a man and a woman stroll across in the same direction: he in a grey bowler and dark grey suit, she in a full-length gown, chestnut-brown, and carrying a lacy parasol, unopened. Two schoolboys stand in the very foreground, just their heads and shoulders visible, with straw boaters and Eton collars. Behind them, the street is busy with more costumed extras, browsing at the market stalls, promenading up and down the street. The impression taken away by any casual viewer of the film, from these few brief seconds, would be of a generalized bustle and activity; the two girls in the bottom left-hand corner would attract no special attention, I suppose. But I have watched and rewatched that fragment of videotape, until the tape itself has grown worn-out and jittery, looking for meaning in those thoughtless gestures, the smiles we exchange, the raising of my hand, the turn of Beatrix's head as she looks away and smiles into the distance, restless, independent. Perhaps it is wrong to look for meaning in such things. Perhaps the meanings we find that way are treacherous and false, like the wind in which my hair seems to wave, which was not a real wind at all, but came from a huge machine set up about fifty yards away, powered by cables which coiled and trailed around the street like a nest of snakes.

It's certain, at least, that we both look ecstatically happy. Baby Thea was at Warden Farm, being looked after by her grandparents (or more likely a member of their staff), and her absence always seemed to lift Bea's spirits. That's a shocking thing to say, isn't it? But quite true. Furthermore, we were being paid for our day's work: one pound and ten shillings each, an absolutely colossal sum in those days. With that money, I was able to buy myself any new book that I wanted, for more than a year afterwards! The whole town was suffused with a sort of carnival atmosphere. There were spotlights, cables and reflectors everywhere. Normal life was impossible and indeed had been abandoned by almost everyone. One or two unimpressed tradesmen and shopkeepers refused to cooperate and would not remain silent when the cameras were turning. There were a number of retakes on that account, and some angry words exchanged. The whole process, I remember, was extremely slow. It took most of the day just to achieve that particular shot, and there were long hours of standing about waiting for the sunshine. The crew seemed to find these delays boring; I was happy for them to go on for ever. Of course I was not brave enough to speak to Jennifer Jones herself: in fact the first time I glimpsed her, in the flesh, I almost fainted. She was only a few feet away from me, in full costume, and was chatting quite naturally and unaffectedly, not to a fellow actor or crew member, but to one of the townspeople! I suddenly felt guilty, and somehow . . . *filthy* (that sounds excessive, I know, but it is the truth) for having kept that picture under my pillow for so long, for having made a fetish of it like that. It seemed to take away my entitlement to have a normal conversation with her. She was wearing an ankle-length skirt, grass-green, with double pleats at the ankle and puffs at the sleeve, and a slightly battered straw hat which matched the blue of the sky and was circled with worn and faded orange roses. I think the point of the costume was to emphasize the contrast between her character's dress, which was meant to be newly bought, and the hat, which was not. Her figure looked stunning in this dress, but I learned afterwards this was partly because she had spent hours getting herself squeezed into an incredibly tight corset. She must have been in agony. Anyway, despite being too shy to say anything to her, I was happy to spend the time between takes just bathing in her presence, in her proximity. She was every bit as beautiful in real life as on the screen; in fact more so, because, in repose, there was a kind of sadness to her expression, as if some settled melancholy had started to engrave itself upon her, and this somehow gave her face more character than it had seemed to wear in her photographs. I could not take my eyes off her.

Beatrix, however, had found another way of occupying herself. Inside the buttermarket, last-minute work was still being carried out on some of the props and sets. In particular, they were busy putting the finishing touches to the market stall where Jennifer Jones's character would soon be having a conversation with her cousin in one of the later scenes, and already Beatrix had managed to strike up quite a friendship with one of the carpenters there. He was not a local man – his name was Jack, and he had come up with the crew from London, where he had been working for some months at Shepperton studios. Beatrix would fetch him pints of beer from the George and Dragon and then they would share them, leaning together on the counter of the market stall and losing themselves in silly, flirtatious chat.

I had better cut short what is rapidly turning into a very long story. In a matter of days, the production had moved on from Much Wenlock to Church Stretton, so that they could start filming in the real Shropshire hill country. My time at Beatrix's house came to an end, and I took the train back home. I had enjoyed the experience – enjoyed it more than just about anything that had happened to me in recent years – but I could see that the film-making world was a different world to my own, one in which I did not altogether belong or feel comfortable. I was still a very withdrawn and awkward girl. To have stood in the street next to Jennifer Jones was, of course, something I could never have pictured even in my most out-rageous fantasies, and I knew that I would never forget it (which has turned out to be true), but in spite of that, the life these people seemed to lead looked fragile and unreal to me. And although everyone connected with the film had been welcoming, and friendly, I did not mistake those qualities for anything else: I knew that when the filming was over, the two worlds would separate, life – routine, everyday life – would return to that corner of Shropshire, and the gods would move on, to whichever exalted place their orbit carried them next, without a single regret or a backward glance. That was the natural order of things.

With Beatrix, it was quite different. Her head had been completely turned by these events, and there could be no going back. For the next few weeks, she followed the crew wherever they went, first of all to the hill country and then to Shrewsbury, where they set up a makeshift studio in a disused aerodrome. If she could not leave Thea with her husband, she would leave her with someone else, or, as a last resort, she would take her along. She became a familiar bystander and hanger-on (and appeared in one or two more crowd scenes, I believe, although I have never been able to spot her). And she spent as much time as possible talking to Jack.

This is how I imagine it happened. One day, he would have asked her if she could guess how much he was being paid for his work on the film. She would have named some extravagant sum, and he would have shaken his head, looking at her teasingly. Then he would have taken her on to the set, and he would have shown her the caravan.

It was a real old gipsy caravan, solid and beautifully made. He had been restoring it, and painting it, and it was now a festive riot of yellow and blue stripes.

It was going to be used as the backdrop to one of the key scenes in the film, after nightfall at the Shropshire County Fair. And this, no less, was the payment he had negotiated for himself. When work on the film was finished, he was going to keep this caravan, buy himself a horse and set off on a voyage of exploration. He was a free spirit and he had been doing other people's work for long enough. It was time to do something for himself.

'Where will you be going?' Beatrix would have asked, mightily impressed. And he would have answered: 'To Ireland.' Yes, he was going to trek around Ireland in a gipsy caravan. Could anything have been more ludicrously romantic? All he needed to complete the escapade, when you think about it, was a companion: a female companion, obviously, one who was pretty enough to look good sitting beside him on the front seat of that caravan and who shared his sense of adventure, his willingness to break out of the shackles of convention. Until now, he had not had the good fortune to find this person. But now, suddenly, his luck was in. The search was over.

Let me look at the lobby card my friend sent me. It is a good picture of her, of Jennifer Jones. In this scene, her character is having difficulty resisting a par-ticularly strong seduction attempt from the villainous squire. The squire, played by David Farrar, has his back to the camera. The only clue to his character, in this picture, is offered by his shoulders, which are broad and masterful. His position towards her is domineering. Her face is soft and vulnerable. She is pleading with him, wordlessly, not to throw temptation in her path like this. She is drawn to him, but also repulsed. Why repulsed? The film never really explains that, except by making it clear that he is wicked. Jack was not wicked – not by any means, so far as I know. Nonetheless, it was not a good decision, on Beatrix's part, to throw in her lot with him and his gipsy caravan. Perhaps it was just something she had to get out of her system. You can see a good part of the caravan here, behind the two incipient lovers. I was mistaken about the blue and yellow stripes – there are green ones, as well. Not that it matters. There are two candleholders on either side of the front door, with torches burning brightly in them. Does it help you, Imogen, to understand any of this, if I describe so minutely the things that you will never be able to see? Does it help you to understand why your grandmother walked out on your grandfather in the autumn of 1949, and took your infant mother along with her, and dragged her round Ireland in a gipsy caravan for more than three years?

I don't know whether it does or it doesn't. I can only give you the facts, after all. The facts of what I see before me, and the facts of what I remember, or believe that I do. I remember Beatrix leaving, anyway. I remember my mother receiving the news from her sister Ivy, on the telephone, and then telling me. I remember being terribly hurt that Beatrix had not troubled to tell me herself. But then it was all done in great haste. The first that Roger knew about it, so the story went, was when he came home from work one day and found that both his wife and daughter were missing. Goodness only knows what he must have felt, when the realization broke upon him. Relief, I suppose! Certainly he never made any attempt to follow them. He was free again, sooner than he could have dared to hope. To a man like him, that could only have been a blessing.

A postcard, now, for picture number nine. The only postcard that Beatrix ever sent me, in all the years that she was away in Ireland.

'Brandon Bay', the caption says, in handwritten capital letters, in the bottom left-hand corner of the card. I have never been to Brandon Bay, or indeed to Ireland. It is somewhere on the Dingle peninsula, I believe. But I still know this landscape well. In fact I do not even need to look at the postcard to describe it to you. In my bedroom at my parents' house in Bournville I worked at a little school desk. It was here, in the early months of 1950, that I sat every night doing my homework and working for my School Certificate. I pinned this photograph on to the wall, in front of me – a wall that was otherwise covered with revision timetables, lists of dates from history and quotations from Shakespeare and others. It was the one little bit of escapism I allowed myself. My mother did not approve, because the postcard was from Beatrix, and Beatrix had disgraced herself and the family (yes, people still thought like that, in those days) by abandoning her husband and running off with another man. But still, she did not try to stop me from pinning the picture to my wall. She knew that, where Beatrix was concerned, my loyalty could not be shaken.

The colours have survived the last half-century remarkably well. The greens and golden yellows of the mountains are still strong and vivid. The ocean looks pale – grey rather than blue – but I believe it must always have looked that way. The photograph was taken from high up on a mountain overlooking the bay, on a day when the sky was overcast, a flurry of cumulus clouds. In the foreground, there is an outcrop of rocks, jutting out of the thick grass, and then this outcrop dwindles away into an archipelago of smaller, broken-up rocks scattered down the side of the mountain, as if a giant had tossed them there. The sweep of the mountain down to the bay is quite gentle, taking you across a mile or so of intermingled greens, browns and yellows – all uncultivated, and quite barren, with what seem to be the ruins of a cottage somewhere in the middle – and then sweeping down to the water's edge. The sea lies placid and unmoving, and behind it, thrusting itself forward, is another shoulder of land, tapering into a spear-like strip of beach. A window of pale blue sky, the palest blue imaginable, is just opening or closing between the clouds. In the far distance is the hint, no more, of another bay, and beyond that, more land, an island perhaps, just the faint intimation of its shadowy bulk, rising up and falling back into the water like the body of some enormous whale or sea-monster.

On the reverse of the postcard were a few words which I have also committed to memory. They were:

'Dear Ros. Hooray for freedom! The open road and the clear blue sky! I have discovered how to live at long last. Love Bea.'

It was the only message she sent me, and the only contact I had with her, for almost four years. The next time I saw her, I was already at university.

Now, this one brings back some memories, I must say. Picture number ten: a boat on the Serpentine in Hyde Park, and a face I have not looked at for many, many long years: my fiancé, Maurice. And sitting beside him, the woman whom I suppose I must describe as the first, and greatest, love of my life – Rebecca. A unique photograph, I have to say, and one which records a most uncomfortable and ill-advised afternoon.

I was a student at the time. Rebecca and I were both students, although she was in her third year and I was still in my first. We were studying at King's College, London, and I was living in a hall of residence in South Kensington, not far from the Albert Hall. All very thrilling to me, as you might imagine, after almost twenty years in the suburbs of Birmingham.

As for my engagement, that was something I had allowed to happen (my role in it being really no more active than that) just before coming down to London. His name, as I said, was Maurice, and we had met at Bournville tennis club and had 'walked out' together (the phrase will sound impossibly quaint to you, I'm sure) for just a few weeks before he proposed to me. He was my first boyfriend. I suppose that in those days, not being very interested in men, I somehow assumed that they would show no interest in me either. It was such a shock when somebody *did* take an interest that I felt absurdly grateful to him. This gratitude was easily mistaken for something else, and for a while I must genuinely have believed that I was attracted to Maurice. I must even have believed myself to be in love with him. However, this delusion, I am pleased to say, did not endure. I had Rebecca to thank for that.

She was two years older than me, so there were not, in theory, very many reasons for us to meet. The first time was at a party given by mutual friends. I can't remember the occasion, at all. I can only remember a room full of over-earnest young people – a positive sea of cardigans and pullovers, an ocean of wool – and in the midst of it – or, I should more accurately say, on the fringes – someone who clearly did not fit in, someone who had over-dressed for the occasion, misjudged it completely and was standing in a full-length, sleeveless evening gown, hovering on the edges of several groups, but too reserved, it appeared, to break into any of them. I could only marvel at how lovely and glamorous she seemed, compared to these other somewhat nondescript friends of mine. Her shoulders were exquisite. At the same time, I am ashamed to say, I rather despised her for her shyness and decided not to approach her, even though I was convinced that she was trying to catch my eye. And so we remained in this somewhat ridiculous situation for the next two hours, eyeing each other up surreptitiously, but neither of us brave or generous enough to make the leap into conversation.

In retrospect, it's the sort of behaviour you might expect from two potential lovers. Needless to say, this reflection did not occur to me at the time.

I saw Rebecca many times over the next few weeks, but usually at a distance, or in a crowded lecture theatre, or busy refectory. If I had taken the opportunity to speak to her on the first of these occasions and said something banal but friendly, such as, 'Not much of a party the other night, was it?', then we would have got started much sooner. Something always seemed to stop me, and yet nothing (I realized, after a while) seemed to stop me from thinking of her, or looking out for her. It rapidly became apparent to me that I was, in some sense that I couldn't or wouldn't define, obsessed with her.

As one can see from this photograph, Rebecca had blonde hair, not quite shoulder length. She was very tall, and her skin was pale, with a hint of freckles. Habitually she wore a rather doleful expression – if you caught her offguard, in a private moment, you might think that she looked dejected – but she also had a lively, girlish sense of humour and was easily roused to laughter. When she laughed, her blue-green eyes narrowed to slits and her lips parted widely to reveal two perfect rows of large white teeth. It goes without saying that she seemed to me absolutely, flawlessly beautiful.

When I did finally speak to her, it was on a Friday afternoon. Maurice was coming down for the weekend, and I was running out of Hall on my way to meet him at Euston station. She was standing near the front door, looking at one of the noticeboards. I was late and in a dreadful hurry. None the less, impelled as if by some magnetic force, I paused, altered my route and went over to stand by her. She was reading the flyer for some forthcoming concert, and I pretended to be interested in it too. I stood so close to her that I almost touched her shoulder, causing her to turn and look at me. It may have been my imagination but I was convinced that, when she saw who it was standing beside her, her eyes lit up, briefly, involuntarily, and a smile flitted across her face. It would be impossible, now, not to say anything to her, so I stumbled out some words. 'Looks interesting, doesn't it?' I was referring to the concert, although I had barely glanced at the flyer, and had no idea which works were being performed. She answered: 'Yes. I think I might go along.' She asked me if I already had a ticket, and when I said that I hadn't, she said that she would buy two. And that was that. The whole exchange had taken about ten seconds. But when I walked away, and out into the busy street, it already felt as though my life had been turned around and set in a completely new direction.

That was a strange weekend, a weekend of mixed feelings. Excitement – an entirely irrational excitement, which I never allowed myself to analyse – at the prospect of an evening spent with Rebecca, mingled with irritation (there is really no other word) with Maurice and all his ways. We had been seeing each other for about three months, by now, and had been engaged for almost half that time. Of course, when he came down to see me for the weekend, he stayed by himself at an hotel, never in my room at Hall. Overnight visits were strictly forbidden by the university authorities. I once suggested, teasingly, that I should smuggle him in after the eleven o'clock curfew, but he was profoundly shocked, and afterwards I realized, on reflection, how relieved I was that he hadn't taken me up on it. It was such a pleasure, I'm ashamed to say, after kissing him goodnight on the main steps, to feel the front door shutting between us, and to walk up the stairs to my room, alone. Free, and autonomous. All the same, we spent a lot of time together on those weekends, and got to know each other's habits pretty well. Too well, as a matter of fact. I vividly remember a stupid argument we had over table manners. I accused him of making too much noise by scraping his knife across the plate while he was eating. It was setting my teeth on edge. What was really setting my teeth on edge, needless to say, was the fact that I was sitting having dinner with Maurice at all, when my head was already full of Rebecca. The feeling was unbearable, literally unbearable. I don't know what stopped me from walking out on him there and then. But it's amazing how long one can stay in denial, over certain things.

The concert was on a Tuesday night, and was held in Grosvenor Chapel in South Audley Street. Rebecca and I met outside St George's Hospital on Hyde Park Corner. The first thing she told me was that the concert had sold out, and that she had been unable to buy tickets. But I was not to worry, apparently, because she knew the woman who was taking tickets on the door (a fellow student), and had been told that we could come in, without paying, and stand listening at the back.

It was a winter's night – I suppose we must be talking about early December 1952 – very blustery and bitterly cold. I haven't been to London now for about five years, and the last time I went, I thought it a most noisy and stressful and disagreeable place; whether you are familiar with it or not I have (of course) no idea. But I can assure you that it was a very different city in the early 1950s. For one thing, wherever you looked, the signs of war damage, and subsequent attempts at reconstruction, were everywhere. It may seem a strange thing to say, but to someone like me – because I have always had rather *romantic* habits of mind – this made the city seem somehow picturesque and ... well, *enchanted*, in a curious kind of way. A fine snow was falling, resting briefly on the surface of things like a light dusting of icing sugar on a cake, and that, of course, made the scene more magical still. Perhaps it was just the mood I was in. It was also, at this time of night, and in this part of Mayfair at any rate, uncommonly quiet: I can remember the echo of our footsteps in the street far more clearly than anything we said to each other. What did we talk about, anyway? Personal details, I suppose, would have tumbled out – places of birth, what we were studying, family details: fairly banal information, but all delivered in the tremulous, confiding tones you always hear when lovers are conversing for the first time.

Of course, we were not lovers yet, nor did we become so that night. Not in the physical sense, at any rate. On the other hand, I (I cannot speak for Rebecca, after all, certainly not at so many years' distance) was without doubt deeply in love by the time we said goodnight to each other. I lay awake for most of the night, thinking of the concert, how we had stood together, surreptitious and conspiratorial, at the very back of the church, enjoying the music but at the same time detached from it (I seem to remember a Bach cantata), the flicker of candlelight all around us, reflected in her eyes, making them dance, her already gilded hair approaching something like incandescence (or so it seemed to me, anyway, in my state of youthful rapture). I thought about her voice, having expected something plummy, Home Counties, like someone you would hear on the BBC Home Service. But instead, her accent was West Country, with lengthened vowels and a wry intonation. She was down-to-earth, and funny. We had whispered jokes to each other, lips against each other's ears, while everyone else in the audience listened to the music in solemn, loveless silence. I curled up tighter in the warmth of my bed, hands between my knees, hugging the memory to myself. And at the same time, a kind of dread was hovering, at the edges of my thoughts, the knowledge that something uncharted and dangerous was being offered to me. But I pushed this dread away, refused to acknowledge it.

The next weekend, I had arranged to go up to Birmingham, to see my parents and of course to spend some more time with Maurice. I hated the very thought of it. But went, all the same. One night – probably the Saturday night – he came round for dinner at my parents' house. In the silence of their kitchen, the scraping of his knife against the plate seemed even louder than ever. Afterwards, we sat around the table with my mother, and he brought out a glossy brochure and a set of architect's drawings. I didn't understand at first, until I realized that these were the plans for a house, one of two dozen or more identical houses on an estate which had not even been built yet. This house was only now in the early stages of construction, and already, without consulting me, he had bought it! I remember being speechless, and crying tears of fury in bed that night. But still I didn't say anything. I could see no alternative to Maurice, even though images of Rebecca kept rising up before me, unbidden, all the long sleepless night.

Why I decided that it would be a good idea for Maurice and Rebecca to meet, I have no idea. I must have known that it would be an awkward occasion, and I can only suppose that, subconsciously, some demon was working within me, with the ulterior motive of forcing a crisis out of a situation that was rapidly becoming intolerable. It was early on a Sunday afternoon, towards the very end of that Christmas term, I imagine. We met for coffee at Daquise, a Polish restaurant in South Kensington, and afterwards strolled up towards Hyde Park.

It was Maurice's idea, I recall, to hire a row boat and take it out on the Serpentine. Doubtless he wanted to show off his prowess as an oarsman to not just one but two admiring young ladies. It was not such a chivalrous idea after all, however, since those of us who were not rowing were in danger of freezing to death. But he meant well, as always.

Let me look closely at the photograph, now. Fifty-three years ago, good grief. I wonder whatever became of Maurice. He was eight or nine years older than me, so this photograph would capture him in his late twenties. A thick, herringbone overcoat, with what appears to be a single-breasted tweed suit beneath it. The inevitable tie. Round, hornrimmed spectacles, framing a pair of beady eyes. A rounded, protuberant chin. On his head, a trilby hat, tipped back at what he no doubt considered to be a jaunty angle, revealing a 'V' of slicked-back auburn hair, slightly receding. I must try not to be unkind about

Maurice, because he was not a bad man, and he was not unattractive. Probably he ended up by making somebody a decent husband. In any case, most people would hardly notice him when they looked at this picture. It's Rebecca who predominates, who holds the attention. This is partly to do with her height – she is a full six inches taller than him – partly with the extraordinary blondeness of her hair: this photograph is somewhat overexposed, or perhaps it has been left in the sun; at any rate, you can see that the colours might have been quite crude and lurid, once, in the manner of photographs from that era, but they have since been bleached out, and now Rebecca's hair is almost white, and almost luminescent, giving off light like the halo around one of the seraphim in a Renaissance painting. She is wearing a navy-blue coat. I remember this coat; she wore it constantly. This photograph only shows her from the waist up, but it was a long coat, reaching below the knee, and she usually wore slacks with it. She preferred trousers to skirts, on the whole. That sleeveless dress she was wearing, the first time I saw her at the party, was untypical. She had the peculiar knack of dressing like a man yet remaining entirely feminine.

Looking at the cloudless sky, and the way that they are both squinting slightly at the camera, you can tell that it was a good, crisp, bright winter's day. They are both smiling. A neutral observer, coming to this picture with no prior knowledge of the people involved, or the situation they found themselves in, would probably read nothing much into these smiles. Both parties seem to be enjoying themselves. But oh, the tension and uncertainty that was in the air that afternoon! It was very cruel of me, in retrospect, to bring the three of us together. Maurice probably had the best time, because he had no intimation, of course, of what Rebecca and I were beginning to feel for each other. It was simply way beyond the reach of his experience or imagination. Whereas poor Rebecca herself (she told me this much later) was in torment. Her feelings for me were at their earliest, most tender and vulnerable stage, and to be forced to bottle them up for hours like this, and watch powerless while Maurice asserted all his usual claims over me – taking my arm, kissing me, and so on … It must have been quite dreadful for her. When we said goodbye a little later, near the Albert Memorial, she stormed off down Queensgate without looking back. I remember wanting to run after her, and I remember Maurice's hand on my arm, detaining me. Perhaps he had realized, by then, that he was engaged in a battle for power, although he can't have believed that it was a very serious one. He must have been confident that the odds were stacked in his favour. He must have sensed victory – or, more than that, believed in his very marrow that it was his by divine right.

Well, Maurice was mistaken, unfortunately.

Two days after that Sunday, I broke off the engagement. I am afraid I did it in rather a cowardly manner, by letter. In any case, if I had hoped to avoid a confrontation this way, I was being naive. Maurice came down by train again two days later and turned up at my room in Hall. He must have taken a very early train from Birmingham because his hammering on the door woke me out of a deep sleep. At first I would not let him in. Finally, however, I had no choice, because the indignity of having the details of our relationship shouted out from the other side of a closed door, for the whole college to hear, was too much to bear. When I unlocked the door he burst into the room looking pale and feverish, his hair in wild disarray, like a mad thing. But he did not stay for long. Doubtless he had many things that he wanted to say to me but when he saw that Rebecca was lying in my bed, naked, he stared at her disbelievingly for a few seconds, then turned on his heels and left. He never spoke to me again after that. It was an unfortunate way to end the affair, on the whole.

Normally I don't like photographs of formal occasions. They are even more mendacious than usual. This next picture – number eleven, I think, in our series – is a good example, because although it seems to record an occasion with perfect fidelity, it actually gives no indication of what was going through the minds of the people who were there. There is, if you like, the 'official' interpretation of the picture, and behind it, there is the unofficial, authentic version. On the one hand, it is a photograph of Rebecca's graduation ceremony; on the other, it is a picture of Rebecca and me in the few hours following our first serious quarrel.

It was taken outside the Albert Hall, where the ceremony was held, so we are not far from the location of the last photograph, not far at all. Rebecca is standing between her parents, and I am on the right-hand side, next to her mother, but slightly removed from the group. I can't remember who took this one, exactly – one of Rebecca's fellow graduates, we must presume. I had been introduced to Rebecca's parents as her 'friend', and they seemed to accept this designation at face value. She had just gained a good honours degree in history and was about to start work as an archivist at the General Register Office at Somerset House; we had found a flat to share together on the first floor of a Victorian conversion in Putney, while I completed my degree; the whole arrangement must have seemed perfectly normal and desirable. Such was the innocence of those times (or so it seems now), and such was the impeccably bourgeois world-view of Rebecca's mother and father, that no other likely interpretation would have occurred to them. If they had observed our behaviour towards each other that day a little more closely, however, surely the seeds of a suspicion might have been sown. If we were 'just' friends, they might have asked themselves, then why on earth were we so cross with each other?

I'm looking at the picture carefully now, to see if any trace of that crossness made its way on to our faces. Rebecca's first. She looks very silly, as everybody does on their graduation day, wearing one of those ludicrous mortar boards with dangly tassels and carrying a big scroll of parchment which she doesn't know where to put. She is smiling in a very self-conscious way, but I'm sure that has less to do with crossness than with knowing how foolish she looks. Her parents are beaming, fulsomely. Is that the right word? You talk about 'full beam', don't you, when describing a car's headlights. Well, that's them, in this photograph: they are on full beam. Today, everything is for the best, in the best of all possible worlds, as far as they are concerned. He is broad, short and dark, she is tall, blonde and thin: fortunately Rebecca took after her mother. They were a most ill-suited couple, the kind of couple I always assume will separate as soon as their children have left home. Whether they did so, I have no idea. They liked me at first, embraced me as a friend of their daughter and then, when the peculiarity of our domestic arrangements became more and more apparent (you will understand what I mean by that shortly), they became increasingly hostile to me. Actually, *he* became increasingly hostile – I don't think that she cared a fig what was going on, so long as her daughter was happy. A much more mature outlook, in my opinion. Anyway.

I am still wearing my hair long, in this picture. Rebecca liked it that way; she was furious with me when I had most of it chopped off a few months later. It is quite wild and unruly: we must have left the flat in such a hurry that I had time to do nothing more than stick a couple of pins into it. As for my jacket, I remember it well: my mother had bought it for me in Rackham's in Birmingham, just before I came down to London, and we both considered it the height of fashion. It was light grey and had three-quarter-length sleeves and radiating tucks at the shoulder. In this picture I am wearing it with a very pretty skirt: a wide pleated swing skirt, with a broad front panel and a pattern of deep red roses against a white background. The hemline is just below the knee. Ah, but look what you can see beneath the skirt, just above my left ankle! A huge ladder in my stocking. That was probably something I had done in my agitation, that morning. There was no way I would have allowed myself to appear in public with a ladder like that, unless we had both come out in a terrible state of fluster and confusion.

Well then, let me tell you something about the quarrel. To be honest, the atmosphere in our flat had been strained – and that is putting it mildly – for a couple of days. Perhaps I should describe the flat to you, first of all. It was furnished, after a fashion: plain, cheap, uncomfortable furniture. There was one bedroom, containing a double bed, and there was also a foldaway single bed in the sitting room. It was our landlady's assumption, obviously, that we would sleep separately, and we never saw any need to disabuse her. Off the sitting room was a tiny kitchenette, barely large enough for the two of us to stand in at once. The sitting room itself was entered by a communal hallway; there were two other flats in the house, and we all shared the same bathroom and toilet. These were all perfectly adequate living arrangements, for two ladies sharing. If Rebecca and I had been able to occupy the flat that way – just the two of us – then I'm sure we would have been quite comfortable. However, it was not to be. In fact we only ever spent about three weeks there, together and alone, before being joined by someone else.

We had no telephone. The first I knew of what was

about to happen was when the electric bell to our flat shrilled late one summer evening, two nights before Rebecca's graduation. This was in July 1953, and it was just getting dark, so I suppose it must have been round about nine o'clock. Rebecca went downstairs to see who was at the front door and when she came back up she had two people with her, two people I was not expecting to see: Beatrix and Thea.

Thea was by now not quite five years old. One of the first things that became apparent was that she was extremely tired, so we boiled up some milk and made her a mug of hot cocoa and then put her to sleep in our double bed. While we did this I remember Beatrix sitting on the sofa looking apprehensive, squeezing her hands together in a nervous gesture.

Of course I was very surprised to see her, and she seemed surprised that I was surprised. She asked me if I had not received her telegram, and I said that I hadn't. Then she realized that she had forgotten to send it. It was at this point that it occurred to me she was in a very agitated state. We had no alcohol in the flat, but Rebecca went downstairs and borrowed a bottle of brandy from our landlady, with whom we were still, in those days, on good terms. We poured Beatrix a generous glassful and while we were at it, I seem to remember, had a small glass ourselves. It was a disturbing situation, and all our nerves were frayed.

The full story did not emerge that evening: we heard only the beginnings of it. Beatrix and Jack, in any case, had separated – that much I could have guessed for myself. The adventure was over, the flames of passion had fizzled out, and the gipsy caravan – now a rotten and bedraggled shadow of its former self – had been sold off to a scrap dealer in Dublin. They had had a good run of it, really: a romantic escapade they had managed to stretch out for three years, during which time Beatrix had written to me only once, on the postcard which I have already described to you. Given this lack of contact, my feelings upon seeing her again so suddenly were mixed, to say the least. She and Thea had been in London for a few days, she said, staying at an hotel. Earlier that day she had telephoned my parents, and they had given her my new address. Since returning from Ireland, she had not visited Warden Farm, or attempted to contact her mother and father.

We put Beatrix into our bed with her daughter, and managed to muddle up some sleeping arrangement for ourselves in the sitting room. I may have slept on the floor, I can't quite remember. Neither of us had a very good night's sleep, that's for sure.

Rebecca went out the next morning. Her parents were arriving in London by train; she went to meet them at the station and then spent the day with them, taking them to Lyons Corner House, the National Gallery, all the usual sorts of things. In the evening they took her out to dinner, so I had the opportunity to spend the whole day alone with Beatrix and Thea. At one point we went out and walked across Putney Bridge to Bishop's Park. We took the river path down to the children's playground, and it was there, while Thea was temporarily occupied with the swings and slides, that Beatrix told me of her latest dilemma.

There was a new man, of course. 'Rosamond,' she announced, 'I am in love.' 'Congratulations,' I answered. I thought of telling her that I was in love too, but decided against it. 'His name is Charles,' she said. 'He's from Canada. He lives in Vancouver.' I could see, immediately, that this situation might entail some inconveniences. It was no surprise when she declared her intention of following him to Vancouver at the earliest opportunity. 'I'm leaving tomorrow night,' she said. 'I've booked a flight to Toronto.' This was an astonishing statement. We were living in the age before jet travel: transatlantic flights were by no means as commonplace as they are now, and they were impossibly expensive. I never did find out (or ask) where she found the money to finance this latest trip. Anyway. I was more interested in the fact that she had just spoken in the first person singular. '*I'm* leaving tomorrow night,' she had said. Not '*we*'. 'What about Thea?' I asked, and she replied: 'Yes. There is a difficulty there.'

Luckily, however, she had thought of a way of resolving this difficulty: and this, predictably enough, was where I came into the equation. Already she had made things stickier for herself than I could have imagined, because, having met this man Charles in Dublin, ingratiated herself with him, hopped into bed with him and goodness knows what else – despite all this, she had somehow neglected to mention to him that she was the mother of a four-year-old daughter. 'Who was looking after her,' I asked, 'while this was going on?' She told me that Jack had been taking care of Thea – which, I have to say, seemed very obliging of him, in the circumstances. Jack, she insisted, was devoted to Thea – had become like a father to her. For the last few weeks, apparently, he had been spending the evenings looking after Thea in the small Dublin boarding house that had been their temporary home, under the happy impression that Beatrix was hard at work, waiting tables in the Castle Hotel, while in fact she had been out carousing and canoodling with this Canadian businessman whom she had met on her second night there. When this discrepancy came to light, there was – as you might suppose – an almighty row, and that was that. The end of the affair. They had parted on terms of such acrimony that there was no question of their maintaining contact any longer, and Thea, in the process, had lost a valuable father-figure, although nobody seemed to be saying anything about that. Meanwhile Charles had returned to Vancouver, and it had now become Beatrix's mission in life to follow him there and secure her place in his heart.

'I *have* to be with this man,' she insisted. 'He means everything to me. Now that we've met, I just cannot bear the thought of life without him.' She seemed confident that he could be made to return these feelings, if circumstances would only allow them a little more time in each other's company. 'We parted very badly,' she confessed. 'He could see that I was not being honest with him, that I was withholding something. I've had time to think about the situation now, and I see that I handled it wrongly, and now I know exactly what to do. If I can go over there, and explain about Thea, then I'm sure everything will be all right. Honesty is the only possible way forward.' I opened my mouth to speak, but she stopped me. 'I know what you are going to say,' she exclaimed. 'I know, it would have been far easier to do all this in Dublin.' This was not, in fact, what I had been going to say. I had been about to suggest that at this point, now that the horse had bolted, so to speak, perhaps a telephone call would be a quicker and cheaper way of moving the situation forward. But I could see that I would be wasting my breath. Beatrix clearly felt that she had a big job of persuasion to do, and that, among her methods of persuasion, she would be obliged to employ some that were not entirely verbal. It was fairly obvious what she had in mind. Equally obvious was the fact that Thea would have to stay behind in England for the time being, and that someone, some trusted friend, would have to look after her.

'Perhaps Thea could stay with her father,' I ventured, but this suggestion was dismissed out of hand. Roger was not in the least interested, apparently, being fully ensconced in a new life – and a new family – with Much Wenlock's Carnival Queen of 1949.

There was only one thing for it, then. 'You want Thea to stay with us?' I asked. 'Here, in our flat?' 'Oh, Ros, that would be *wonderful*,' Beatrix sighed. 'That would be the most marvellous thing anyone has ever done for me.' I took a long breath before asking the next, crucial question: 'For how long?' Beatrix put her head on one side and pouted; she hesitated for many seconds before answering, and as she did so, she looked at me shyly – or should that be slyly – from the corner of her eyes, as if in full knowledge of the outrageousness of what she was about to request. Finally she said: 'Rosamond, darling, I know this is a terrible, enormous favour to ask, but could you manage for . . .' (I waited, mesmerized) ' . . . two weeks? Or even three?'

In fact, knowing Beatrix as I did, this request did not strike me as very outrageous at all. I had been expecting much worse. To make me feel that way was part of her genius, I suppose. In any case, as I turned away and looked at little Thea, skimming down the tiny slide and then running up the ladder to skim down it again, with robotic regularity and a look of fierce concentration on her face, my heart melted. It would be impossible for anyone not to love this child, you would have thought. Of course I could look after her for that time – perhaps even longer. I clasped Beatrix warmly by the hand and assured her that, if Rebecca agreed with me, she could certainly trust us with the care of her daughter.

Whether Rebecca *would* agree, I had no idea.

Naturally, I did not have to wait long to find out. She came back from dinner that night rather early – at about ten o'clock. Beatrix and Thea had already gone to bed. I poured Rebecca one of those brandies for which we were rapidly starting to develop an appetite, and told her of Beatrix's request.

She stared at me in silence for a few moments. 'You didn't say yes?' she asked. 'Of course not,' I replied. 'I said, "Yes, if Rebecca agrees."' 'Well I don't,' she said, decisively, then finished her brandy and stormed off to the bathroom.

On her return I attempted to reason with her. I pointed out that it would only be for a short period of time, and that Beatrix was not just my cousin, but my oldest friend. All to no avail. 'Forget it,' she said. 'I'd like them both out of this flat first thing tomorrow morning.' More words were spoken – harsher words – and the upshot was that Rebecca spent that night in the sitting room by herself, while I retreated to the darkened bedroom and sat down on the double bed, weeping. Beatrix put out a hand in the dark and rested it on my leg. Thea slept on.

'Poor darling,' Beatrix murmured, soothingly. 'I've got you into trouble with your friend, haven't I?' I nodded and took my clothes off down to my under- wear and got into bed on the far side, so that the sleeping Thea lay between us. Beatrix stretched out her hand, and we held hands over the little girl's body. I remember her sighing and rustling over in her sleep. After a while Beatrix sniffed (I think she had been crying too) and said, 'I'm an awful nuisance, aren't I? You must be livid with me, just turning up like this.' 'I don't mind,' I said; which was the truth.

Well, it is no good pretending I can remember all of our conversation like this. In any case, I suspect that we spent much of the next few hours in silence, wide awake but not talking to one another. I do remember Beatrix saying something to me, at one point, about how close Rebecca and I seemed – 'almost,' she added, insinuatingly, 'almost as if you were *more* than friends'. I said nothing to that, but my heart beat a little faster when she went on, in a tone of even greater mock-innocence: 'I'm sure your mother and father would be *awfully* pleased to know that you have someone like that in your life. Someone with whom you can share absolutely everything.' I wondered what to make of these words, and what to make of the shine I could see in Beatrix's eyes as I glanced over at her in the semi-dark. She glanced back at me and took my hand again and squeezed it and then, staring up at the ceiling, where shadows from the elm tree in the garden were drifting in hazy moonlit patterns, she said: 'Do you remember ...?' She didn't need to continue. I did it for her. 'The night in Shropshire?' I answered, dreamily. 'When we both tried to escape.' 'Such a long time ago,' she said, breathing the words rather than speaking them. 'So much has happened since then. And yet ...' Again, I knew what she was going to say. 'Yes,' I answered. 'Sometimes it feels as though it was only yesterday.'

More than that, as a matter of fact: suddenly it seemed to me that that evening, that wonderful, terrifying adventure, did not belong to the past at all: it felt as though I was living through it again, at that very moment. Beatrix and I were not lying side by side in bed, but beneath the spreading branches of the trees at the edge of Uncle Owen's fields; the motionless figure between us was not Thea, but my little dog Shadow, clutched tightly to my chest. Beatrix put her arm behind my neck, and I pressed myself against her, and we lay like that, on our backs, staring up at the stars. A barn owl was hooting, crying out in the night, very close to us. The trees rustled, the undergrowth was restless with hints of subtle, mysterious life. I could feel the warmth of Beatrix's body, the pulsing of blood through the arm at the back of my head. Her sensations became mine. The moon continued to rise, and with a flurry the owl launched into sudden flight, skimming away beneath the branches of the trees. Despite the cold, I was happy here . . .

When I awoke, Beatrix was no longer with me. I sat up and looked around me, my heart pounding. Then I heard her next door in the sitting room, talking to Rebecca. It was morning. I immediately got out of bed and slipped on my dressing gown.

'I know it's your big day,' I said to Rebecca, 'and we've both got to get ready and everything. But I just wanted to tell you that I've made up my mind. Thea is going to stay with us for a few weeks.'

Rebecca stared at me, her lips hardening into a

narrow line. Beatrix put her arms around me and kissed me gratefully. Thea, lying full-length on the floor in her pyjamas, colouring in the squares of a newspaper crossword with red crayon, did not look up. No more was said on the subject.

And that is why, in this photograph, Rebecca looks so cross with me, and why my hair is in such disarray, and why I have a very obvious ladder in my stocking, extending to almost three inches above my left ankle.

Rebecca's anger did not last long, in the end. She loved me too much, in those days, to stay angry with me for any length of time. 'I'm sure it'll be fine,' she conceded, that night, as Thea sat alone at the little table in the sitting room, dipping fingers of toast into the egg we had boiled for her. Beatrix had already said her farewells and left for London airport. 'It might even be fun to have her with us for two or three weeks. We can take her to the seaside and all sorts of things.' I smiled happily. Everything was going to be all right.

It took Beatrix rather longer than expected to achieve her goal in Vancouver, however. She did not return for more than two years.

'Damn,' said Gill, looking at her watch. 'We'd better stop there.'

It was already six-thirty. Outside, it had been dark for almost two hours. The rush-hour traffic had started, swelled up to saturation point and was even now beginning to recede – all unnoticed by the three women high up in Catharine's flat. Gill and Catharine still sat on the ancient, listless sofa; Elizabeth had by now forsaken the swivel chair and was sitting on the floor between them, her back to the sofa, her head resting against her sister's knees. Catharine flicked the remote control at the stereo and the tape clicked off. They said nothing for a while, drawn together in wordless meditation, as the sounds of the world outside slowly re-entered their consciousness and established themselves there, pushing aside the spectral images that Rosamond's narrative had raised.

'Did you know about all this, Mum?' Catharine asked, finally. 'Had Aunt Rosamond told you any of it before?'

'No,' Gill answered. 'No, it's all new to me.'

'But you've seen these pictures, haven't you?'

'Some of them.' Gill was thinking, already, that as soon as she returned home she would have to retrieve all of Rosamond's photograph albums from the attic, where Stephen had already stowed them, and look more closely at the pictures they contained.

'I'd love to visit Warden Farm,' Elizabeth said, dreamily. 'What was it like?'

'It was just as she describes it,' said Gill, rising to her feet and stretching. 'We used to spend Christmas Eve there every year, when I was a little girl. I think Aunt Rosamond was even there one time – and Thea was with her.' She frowned, straining to resurrect a distant memory. 'I can't be sure, but there *was* an older girl there one year, and we didn't quite know who she was. She must have been about seventeen or eighteen. Yes, I think it *would* have been Thea.'

'Can we go there?' Elizabeth asked. 'Next time we come up to see you, can we all drive over?'

Gill found her handbag and rummaged around inside, looking for lipstick. 'There wouldn't be much point. Ivy and Owen handed it down to one of the sons – Raymond, I think – and the farm didn't do well. He sold up, and the last time I went there it was all shuttered and empty. I think someone bought it in the end – tacked a swimming pool on, and all that sort of thing. But it's not the same any more.'

They took a taxi from Primrose Hill to Marylebone. The sisters perched on the foldaway seats, with their backs to the driver, while Gill sat facing them, hemmed in on either side by instrument cases, a small amplifier, a canvas holdall cat's-cradled-full of flexes and cables, and another small flight-case housing some electronic device which she had, so far, been unable to identify. Bright, fleeting amber light from the streetlamps flashed to and fro across her face as she struggled to get comfortable.

'Do you really need all this stuff?' she asked Catharine. 'I thought you were just going to play the flute.'

'Ah, but you haven't heard what she does with her magical gizmo,' said Elizabeth, swollen with sisterly pride. 'Just wait. You'll think there are twelve of her.'

Not understanding this remark, Gill sat back and gazed out of the window, huddling her raincoat around herself as she felt shivers running through her: whether from cold or anticipation she couldn't say. She was nervous on Catharine's behalf, even though she had seen her performing in public plenty of times before; at the same time, this little concert, which might have seemed a momentous prospect a few hours ago, had started to assume less importance since the playing of those tapes. She was sure that Elizabeth and even Catharine were feeling the same thing: that this recital – the whole reason for her coming down to London in the first place – had become little more than an interlude, now, a frustrating interruption to the progress of Aunt Rosamond's story, an unwelcome incursion into the present when they were all suddenly preoccupied with the past, with the gradual unveiling of their family's occult, unsuspected history.

As they drove on towards Cavendish Square, a freezing mist began to descend. It gave London – or at least this quiet, prosperous, solemn corner of London – a ghostly, unfamiliar air. The massive outlines of fine old buildings dissolved into shadows, purplish and inscrutable. Wreaths of mist unfurled in the glimmer of streetlamps, placed at silvery intervals along the length of Wimpole Street. Even though they could see, as they disembarked from the taxi, that a trickle of people had already begun to arrive at the church, there was little traffic here: most of the audience seemed to be coming on foot. They passed by in groups of three or four, clutching coats tightly against the cold. Catharine recognized some of the faces; greetings and hugs were exchanged while her mother and sister unloaded her cases and paid off the taxi driver.

Gill waited outside while her daughters lugged the equipment backstage, then she and Elizabeth entered the church together and made their way down the aisle towards an empty pew. She was conscious, now, of a mounting disorientation, a sense that she was half-removed from her surroundings. Shadows of the past, remembrances, continued to loom over her. This church: a church on a winter's night, in the West End of London, playing host to a concert ... It was hardly likely to be the same one, she supposed, as the church where Rosamond and Rebecca had attended their first concert together (that had been in Mayfair, hadn't it?): but still, the coincidence – if that's what it was – made her skin tingle. She gazed around her at the warm, muted colours, the candlelight glinting off the golden chancel rail, even bringing the figures on the stained glass windows to some sort of deceptive, flickering life, and she felt that the air was charged with something of the same wonder and bewitchment as on the night, more than half a century ago, when those two women had first dared to guess their feelings for each other.

When Catharine began to play, this intimation grew even stronger. She was third on a bill of five students from her music college, all performing to an audience of friends, colleagues and family. First, a pianist, who had chosen something long, dreamlike and unexpectedly melodic by John Cage. This was followed by a brutally modernist piece for solo cello. It then took a few minutes, and some help from two sound engineers – powering up amplifiers and adjusting the height of a microphone stand – before Catharine was ready to step forward. A hush fell upon the audience, who had grown restless, and a little disgruntled, during the setting-up of her equipment. In the near-silence that followed, the hum from Catharine's amplifier was distinctly audible.

After a pause, and a frown of concentration, she began by playing a long, low, single note on her flute. Then she let it hang in the air, and decay.

Then she played another long note – a minor third above the first – and followed it, after a few seconds' silence, with a simple three-note phrase in an apparently unrelated key.

Next, she clicked on her foot pedal, and suddenly, miraculously, the two notes and the phrase she had already played were repeated, and repeated again. She clicked again, and the notes began to blossom and multiply. Chords began to form, and loops of sound were created, shifting in and out of phase with each other, until the air seemed to be filled with a whole ensemble of flutes, over whose uncanny concord Catharine began to improvise quiet, tentative, fragmentary melodic lines. The music seemed infinitely sad and eerie, as if it were somehow drifting into the church not just from some remote, unvisited place, but from the distant past. Not for the first time that evening, Gill felt her skin turn to goosebumps, and found herself shivering. She'd heard Catharine playing the work of other composers often enough. But it was twice as thrilling, and ten times stranger, to know that the sounds she could hear now were coming from the imagination of her own daughter, someone whom she herself had once brought into the world. At that moment, she knew that they had never been so close to each other: Gill knew exactly what Catharine was thinking, exactly what images were passing through her mind, with every stretched, pregnant note. The music she was playing was not abstract. It was a soundtrack: the soundtrack to a story they had heard together only a few hours earlier, about two little girls, running away from home, on a winter's night in wartime Shropshire. Catharine was thinking of the hidden path that led to the caravan, the rustle of leaves overhead as Beatrix led her trusting cousin away into the forest, the gaunt and sombre silhouette of Warden Farm standing out blackly in the moonlight. These images, these fitful, antique images, were somehow inscribed into the fabric of her music. Gill could not have been more convinced of the fact, even if her daughter had been trying to describe the scene in words.

She glanced across at Elizabeth, and could see that she was feeling it too. And when the improvisation was over, after around seven or eight haunted minutes, they did not, at first, join in with the audience's vigorous applause. Instead they turned and looked at each other, and Elizabeth saw that, although her mother was smiling, proud and joyful and almost overcome with admiration, her eyes were also gleaming moistly.

Afterwards, along with many of Catharine's friends, they went to a pub in Wigmore Place and waited for her arrival. There were more than twelve of them squeezed around the table, including Daniel, the obscurely untrustworthy boyfriend (who had arrived late for the concert), and the pale, waiflike and rather beautiful redheaded pianist who had played the piece by John Cage.

'That was *amazing*,' Gill said, leaping up and hugging her daughter as soon as she came in. Daniel hurried off to buy her a drink, and Catharine squeezed herself into a corner of the table, to a general chorus of greetings and congratulations.

'That gadget of yours,' said Daniel, when he returned with her pint of Guinness, 'I was trying to work out what it does. Is there a little hard disk in there, or something?'

'Trade secret,' said Catharine, flashing him a flirty smile.

'No, but I imagine everything you play into there – within certain parameters – is recorded instantaneously, and then repeated back, is it?'

The workings of the device were not what interested Gill, so she allowed the conversation to go on without listening too closely. It was soon bogged down in minute and unfathomable technicalities. Elizabeth was looking at her watch.

'Getting tired?' Gill asked.

'No. I was just wondering how soon we could get away. I'm dying to listen to the rest of those tapes.'

'Oh.' Gill was surprised. 'I thought we'd do that tomorrow morning.'

'*What*?' said Elizabeth, turning on her. 'You've got to be joking. We're going back to Catharine's place right now.'

Gill glanced over at her daughter, still deep in ever more specialized conversation with Daniel. 'Are you sure we're invited?' she asked, nodding at them meaningfully.

'Well . . . that's a good point.' Elizabeth looked

doubtful, but only for a moment. 'I'll have a word with her. Don't worry about it.'

It transpired, in any case, that Daniel had to be up early for a seminar the next morning, and had not been planning to go home with Catharine after all. So it seemed there was no obstacle to their returning to Primrose Hill that night, and following Rosamond's story to its conclusion. Gill was worried that this meant she wouldn't get to bed until very late, and wondered if she would find herself locked out of her hotel; but her daughters told her not to fret. 'They have twenty-four-hour porters for that sort of thing,' said Elizabeth knowledgeably. They left just before last orders were called. Daniel stood up to kiss Catharine goodbye: a kiss so ostentatious, and reverent, that Gill (reproving herself, at the same time, for her scepticism) wondered if he was not over-compensating for something. It also struck her that he had not actually complimented Catharine on her performance, but merely taken an interest in the workings of her echo machine, or whatever it was. A thought she would have dismissed as irrelevant, probably, had it not been that – just as she was following her daughters out of the door – she spotted Daniel reseating himself next to the redheaded pianist, and caught the first words that he spoke to her. Which were something like: 'That was one of the most beautiful things I've heard in my life.'

*

Eleven-thirty. They are back in Catharine's flat, at the very top of that austere, lofty Victorian house, the sounds of night-time London forgotten again, far beneath them. A bottle of red wine opened, this time, to fortify them against whatever shocks the remaining tapes hold in store. Some bread, cheese and grapes, laid out on a chopping board on the floor, with knives and plates: but nobody seems to want them. The noise of the plane tree, again, as it taps against the windowpane. The overhead lamp switched off, so that the only light in the room comes from the coal-effect gas fire, turned down low and dancing away cheerfully enough in the grate. That, and the phosphorescent turquoise glow from the display panel on Catharine's stereo system. Kneeling before it, she ejects the latest tape to see whether it needs turning over yet, finds that there is still half of this side left to run; and puts it back into the machine. She crawls over to the fire and sits cross-legged in front of it; checks with her mother and sister that they are ready to start listening; and presses the remote control.

Once again, they hear the onset of hiss, and the ambient noise which tells them that they are back in Shropshire, back in Rosamond's bungalow, back in her sitting room, where she sits surrounded by ghosts and photographs. A prefatory cough, the clearing of a frail, elderly woman's throat, and the flow of narrative resumes.

Number twelve. Ah. This one, Imogen, is probably my favourite picture of all. The memories associated with it are exquisitely happy. Almost painfully so. I hope that I can describe it to you calmly, with some objectivity. I have not looked at this picture – not dared to look at it, to tell the truth – for many years. You will have to give me a moment or two to take it all in, and to compose my thoughts, and my feelings.

Very well. A lake, first of all. Clear blue sky, absolutely cloudless. A rich cerulean blue at the very top of the picture, and then getting paler and paler until the sky is almost white where it brushes the top of the mountains. Mountains in the distance, yes: twin peaks, one on either side of the picture, with a long ridge connecting them, dipping gently in the middle. No snow on these peaks today, although there certainly would be in the winter. At the foot of the mountains pastureland begins, and starts to tumble in green, undulating folds towards the far shore of the lake, broken intermittently by patches of pine forest and, almost hidden away in one valley, you can just see a small village, with the church spire rising proudly from a muddle of clustered white buildings and red roofs. This village, unless I'm much mistaken, would be Murol. For we are in the Auvergne district of France, and it is the height of summer: a long, silent, perfect day in the summer of 1955.

We are looking at Lac Chambon, which lies towards the south of the region. The lake is quite still, and reflects the outline of the mountains with exact, unmoving symmetry, so that if you stare at the picture long enough, it starts to look almost like an abstract study in geometry. Trees line the far shore of the lake, and in the foreground of the picture, occupying most of the top right-hand corner, there are the tangled, intertwining branches of a chestnut tree. This tree overhangs a small shingle beach, beyond which, standing in the water, there are two figures with their backs to the camera: a young girl, about six or seven years old, with fair, slightly brownish hair tied into two pigtails, wearing a swimsuit with pink and white vertical stripes; and next to her, a young woman of about twenty-five, wearing a plain navy-blue swimsuit, and a short white pleated skirt over the top – a tennis skirt, I think, in all probability. The woman has blonde hair – brilliant blonde hair, almost white – which falls just short of her shoulders. She is broad-shouldered and athletic-looking, but also slim, and graceful, with long, slender arms and legs. She is bending slightly, to help the little girl with something: it's not entirely clear what, but I suspect she is trying to teach her how to skim stones. They are both standing a few yards out into the lake. The woman is Rebecca, of course, and the little girl is Thea. The person taking the photograph was myself, and when I took it I was lying in a meadow above the beach, surrounded by long grass and wild flowers. You can see a few of the blades of grass, and the petals of what I take to be yellow saxifrage at the very forefront of the picture, blurred and out of focus.

I should tell you why we were taking our holidays in the Auvergne. The explanation might strike you as rather frivolous, but I hope not. It all began like this. One night at the flat in Putney, after Thea had fallen asleep (we had bought a little camp bed so that she could sleep in our bedroom), Rebecca and I were in the sitting room next door, listening to the wireless. We were tuned to the Third Programme, and they were broadcasting a concert which included, among other items, a selection of Canteloube's famous arrangements of the *Songs of the Auvergne*. I recall, Imogen – and I hope this does not shock you – that during the course of the broadcast we became rather amorous with each other. In fact I don't think we ever made love so tenderly and so ... fiercely as that night. It was ... Well, no doubt the details would be of little interest to you. Afterwards, for both of us, those songs were forever associated with that occasion, but more than that, somehow they became – what is the word? – symbolic? – or do I mean *totemic*? – totemic, I think – of the love between us. There was one song in particular, one of the most famous ones – 'Bailero', it is called, a most beautiful love song, very slow, and very sad – it starts with the woodwind voicing such plangent phrases, while the violins play long, lovely, shimmering chords, and then the soprano's voice enters so unexpectedly, so dramatically, singing this extraordinarily *melancholy* tune ... Oh, it is no use, of course, you cannot describe music in words, perhaps the best thing would be if I simply put that song on to the stereo when I have finished describing this picture, so that you can hear it yourself. I will do that, if I remember.

Long-playing records were a fairly recent invention in those days. I can't even remember if our gramophone was equipped to play them. Most music was still sold on '78' discs, and it was in that form, I am sure, that Rebecca bought a copy of 'Bailero' a few days later. We must have driven the neighbours to distraction, playing it day and night. And, from that time on, it became a favourite pastime of ours, to fantasize about making a trip to the Auvergne, for no other reason than to imbibe some of the spirit of the landscape that had given birth to this glorious music. At first it seemed a far-fetched and impractical proposition. We were still accustoming ourselves to the responsibility of looking after Thea, and the thought of taking her to a foreign country with us seemed daunting, and a little capricious. As it became ever more apparent that Beatrix was in no hurry to return, we were obliged to adjust our circumstances, and to make sacrifices. I discovered that caring for a small child was not compatible with studying for a degree, and I dropped out of university midway through the first term of my second year. Rebecca continued to work, and through her diligence we managed to keep our heads above water, financially, and were more or less able to function as a family unit. One of the biggest problems was the attitude of our landlady, who considered the whole set-up most irregular (which it was) and would frequently torment us with threats – sometimes veiled, sometimes not – of bringing the situation to the attention of the authorities, or even our parents – none of whom knew anything about it, for a good while. She could usually be placated, thankfully, with prompt or even advance payment of rent, so that the worst we ever really had to contend with were her constant scowls of disapproval.

We had little contact with Beatrix, and little idea of her whereabouts. Very occasionally, she would telephone. Even more occasionally, she would write. She sent her daughter presents at Christmas (twice) and remembered her birthday (once). Rebecca and I could certainly have been more energetic, in putting pressure on her to return home and bring an end to what was, from many points of view, a most peculiar and unsatisfactory situation. But we did not do this. We adored Thea, and loved having her with us: it was no more complicated than that. We both knew, obviously, that Beatrix was liable to return home at any time, and take her back. This cloudy prospect hung over us constantly. But I suppose that in our way we grew accustomed to it, until it became simply another of our conditions of living.

In the spring of 1955, Rebecca found that she had saved up enough money to buy a small car, and suddenly the fantasy of our trip to France was turned to reality. Thea was by now settled, quite comfortably, in the local primary school; there seemed to be a real solidity in the relations between us, as a family of three, and we felt quite confident about embarking upon our summer adventure. We set off at the end of July and planned to be away for three weeks.

The car was laden with camping equipment. You cannot see it here, but our tent was white, and very plain, and yet big enough for the three of us to sleep in comfortably. Mostly we stayed at official campsites, but at the very end of the holiday, I remember, we pitched camp, for one night only, right next to this shingle beach on the shores of Lac Chambon, and there we found ourselves quite alone. I don't know who that land belonged to – if anyone – but no one disturbed us the whole time we were there.

Those three weeks in France were undoubtedly the happiest of my life, and everything that was good about them is crystallized in this photograph, and in the song 'Bailero', which never fails to evoke for me images of that lake, and that meadow, where we lay all afternoon amidst the long grass and the wild flowers, while Thea played down by the water. There is nothing one can say, I suppose, about happiness that has no flaws, no blemishes, no fault lines: none, that is, except the certain knowledge that it will have to come to an end. As the afternoon waned, the air grew not cooler, but thicker and more humid. We had been drinking wine, and my head was feeling heavy and sleepy. I must have dozed off, and when I awoke, I saw that Rebecca was still lying beside me, but her eyes were wide open, and there was quick movement behind them, as if she were thinking rapid, private thoughts. When I asked her if everything was all right, she turned and smiled at me, and her gaze softened, and she whispered some reassuring words. She kissed me and rose to her feet and wandered down towards the shore, where Thea was collecting pebbles and sorting them into piles according to some eccentric system of her own.

I came to join them, but Rebecca did not turn round when she heard my footsteps on the shingle. She shielded her eyes and looked towards the mountains and said, 'Just look at those clouds. It will be some rainstorm, if those come our way.' Thea heard this remark: she was always quick to notice changes of mood – it surprised me, every time, to realize what a sensitive child she was, how attuned to grown-up feelings. It prompted her to ask: 'Is that why you're looking sad?' 'Sad?' said Rebecca, turning. 'Me? No, I don't mind summer rain. In fact I like it. It's my favourite sort.' 'Your favourite sort of rain?' said Thea. I remember that she was frowning, and pondering these words, and then she announced: 'Well, I like the rain *before* it falls.' Rebecca smiled at that, but I said (very pedantically, I suppose): 'Before it falls, though, darling, it isn't really rain.' Thea said: 'What is it, then?' And I explained: 'It's just moisture, really. Moisture in the clouds.' Thea looked down and became absorbed, once again, in sorting through the pebbles on the beach: she picked two of them up and started tapping them together. The sound and the feel of it seemed to give her pleasure. I went on: 'You see, there's no such thing as the rain before it falls. It has to fall, or it isn't rain.' It was a silly point to be making to a little girl; I rather regretted starting on it. But Thea seemed to be having no difficulty grasping the concept; rather the reverse – for after a few moments she looked at me and shook her head pityingly, as if it was testing her patience to discuss such matters with a dimwit. 'Of *course* there's no such thing,' she said. 'That's *why* it's my favourite. Something can still make you happy, can't it, even if it isn't real?' Then she ran off down to the water, grinning, delighted that her own logic had won such an impudent victory.

The storm never reached us. We watched it break over the distant mountains, and then pass over to the east, but the shores of that lake managed to escape it. We made ourselves a meal and put Thea to bed. Soon the sky was quite clear again, and the stars glittered above us. The moon threw a path of silver across the still surface of the lake.

While Thea slept, Rebecca and I sat on the edge of

the long grass, just where the meadow sloped away towards the beach. We sat side by side, more glasses of wine in our hands, leaning into one another. My head was on her shoulder. The silence of that place was absolute, almost shocking. It obliged one to talk in whispers.

Rebecca was the first to speak. 'You know what Thea said to you earlier,' she murmured. 'When she said that something can still make you happy, even if it isn't real.' I laughed and said: 'Yes, she's a crafty one, all right.' 'Do you think it's true, though?' Rebecca asked, and there was an odd note of insistence in her voice. I didn't understand her. 'What do you mean?' 'I mean –' Rebecca hesitated, as if full of fear, and as if to voice that fear was somehow to give it shape and substance – 'I mean, *this* isn't real, is it? What we have, the three of us. It's not *real*.' I laid my hand on her thigh and squeezed it. 'You both feel solid enough to me,' I answered. 'Have I been hallucinating all this time?' Rebecca didn't answer; it had been a foolish response. 'What are you getting at?' Again, Rebecca said nothing. She sat beside me for a minute or two, still leaning fondly against me, and then, abruptly, she stood up and walked down to the water. She stood there, alone, her silhouette black and heavy in the moonlight. Her arms were folded, her shoulders tensed. I wanted to follow her but I was shocked by her sudden unhappiness, by the savagery of the fear that seemed to have ambushed her from nowhere. When I did step down to the water's edge beside her, and tried to put my arm around her waist, her whole body seemed rigid and unresponsive. 'Rebecca, this is *real*,' I insisted. 'Of course it is. These have been wonderful times, haven't they, for the three of us?' But when she answered me, it was in a voice I had never heard before: cracked, faltering, stricken with animal grief. 'We won't have her for much longer,' she said. 'It's nearly over. This is the end.'

It's a mystery to me, even now, where this intimation could have come from. Whatever the source, she was proved right, in a matter of weeks. Early in September, I received a letter from Beatrix. She was coming back from Canada, at long last, and in something like triumph, by the sound of it, with Charles in tow. Somehow or other, she had won him over, reconciled him to the existence of Thea, and even persuaded him to take a job in London. Furthermore, they now had a son of their own, called Joseph, born about six months previously. What a relief it would be, for me and Rebecca, to have the burden of looking after Thea finally lifted from our shoulders! That was what she was pleased to tell herself, in any case.

Less than a week after we received this letter, Beatrix had arrived. And less than two hours after she arrived, she was gone. And Thea was gone with her. Utterly bewildered, utterly forlorn: snatched away and thrust into the bosom of a new family. A family of perfect strangers.

Rebecca left a few days later. She did it in the

traditional way – waiting for a time when I was out of the flat, and then clearing out her possessions, and writing a note, which was left propped up for me on the dining table. 'I don't want to be in this place without her any longer,' was all that it said. There was an additional sentiment, implied but not actually written: '*Or with you.*'

So I was quite alone.

Rebecca wrote to me, a few months later, full of remorse. We met up for coffee, but it was a wretched occasion, and neither of us, I think, had the stomach for any more meetings. The last glimpse I had of her was … oh, forty years ago? More, in fact. It was in a London restaurant, but she didn't notice me, so …

Ah well.

All of a sudden, I am feeling very tired, Imogen. Forgive me, but I don't feel like finding that song now, and playing it to you. It is very late, and all I really want to do is go to bed. I shall play it to you some other time. Just so that you can hear it for yourself, the way her voice breaks in upon you … That moment, it always makes me think for some reason of a curtain being drawn back – drawn back to reveal, suddenly, a tableau: the cerulean blueness of the lake; Rebecca and Thea; and me, walking across the meadow to join them again.

So, now it is morning, and I am feeling much better. I am ready to tell you all about picture number thirteen: Beatrix and I, sitting on a bench together, late one summer afternoon, in the grounds of a rest home. The name of this establishment escapes me. I am reasonably certain that I only visited it two or three times.

The year of this photograph, I believe, would be 1959. Her accident was the year before, probably in January or February 1958. Following the accident, Beatrix was in hospital for almost a year. Her neck had been broken, and for a while it was thought that she might not be able to walk again. At this particular home, however, she was being treated not for physical ailments but for mental problems which followed in the wake of the accident.

A heavy, grey and uncompromising Victorian house. That is what you can see in the background. The sky behind is a pale blue, mottled with cirrus clouds. The house is symmetrical, with twin gables at each end, each with a pair of chimneys. The photographer (I believe it was one of the nurses) was standing to the right of the house, towards the edge of the wide front lawn, so we see the main building at an oblique angle, which makes it seem a little friendlier, somehow. There are eight windows on the first floor – I seem to remember one of them belonged to Beatrix's room, which had a decent view over the garden – while on the ground floor there are large bay windows at either end of the house. One of these belonged to the recreation area or common room, where they had a grand piano and a small library. I found it a most restful and appealing house – it seemed positively luxurious, compared to my bedsit in Wandsworth, at any rate – but Beatrix hated it, I remember, regarding it in the light of a prison. I recall that they did some fairly unpleasant things to her there, so one can hardly blame her. Electro-convulsive therapy, and that sort of thing.

She and I are in the foreground of this picture, sitting on a bench towards the back of the lawn, just in front of a wonderful border of red and yellow verbenas. We are both dressed rather formally – I wonder why? I am wearing a navy-blue jacket and long grey skirt. My hair is shorter than ever, now – it almost looks like a man's short-back-and-sides. The difference between myself, here, and how I look in Rebecca's graduation photograph, for instance, is very striking. There is a certain grimness in the way my mouth is set, a sort of resigned fixity in the way I am looking at the camera – which of course I may just be imagining, or exaggerating: and in any case, this would hardly have been a happy occasion, after all. The same could be said about Beatrix, who is wearing a loose, somewhat shapeless and baggy dress, full-length, also in navy blue, with a pattern of tiny flowers in pale blue and green. Her expression is not so much grim, I suppose, as vacant and tired. She has a brace on her neck, which makes her whole posture seem very stiff and awkward. She had to wear that brace for about two years, I seem to remember. Awful for her. One couldn't help but sympathize.

This was how the accident had happened. Beatrix and Charles, as I told you, had married and moved back to England. In addition to Thea and her son, Joseph, they now had a baby daughter called Alice. Charles was working in the City, and they had committed themselves wholeheartedly to the sub-urban lifestyle by taking a big house in Pinner. And one Friday afternoon, Beatrix had been seized by what was, to be honest, an uncharacteristic spasm of maternal generosity: she had decided to give Thea a treat: she told her that she would pick her up from school in the car, instead of making her walk home as usual. At five to three, two hundred yards from the school gates, she slowed down and came to a halt at a roundabout in order to allow another car to feed in from the right. Behind her a lorry, driven by a man who had had four pints of beer with his lunch, failed to anticipate her stopping and drove straight into the back of her car, with terrific force.

Fortunately, both of her other children were at home, in the care of a nanny. Otherwise they might well have been killed. Beatrix was the only person in the car and she was jolted forward at speed. At least she was lucky – if that is ever the right word to use in this sort of context – that the car she was driving was a Volkswagen Beetle. These cars were by no means common in Britain at the time. There was still a residual, deep-seated reluctance on the part of many people to buy anything German. I sometimes wonder if Beatrix had not bought it, in fact, for that very reason: because it was a good way of antagonizing her stuck-up, suburban neighbours. Anyway, it turned out, in one sense, to be the saving of her: if she had been driving a more square-backed vehicle, the lorry would simply have ploughed into it and crushed it; but because the back end of her Volkswagen was rounded, the lorry actually mounted it, and the impact was very slightly diminished.

Word of the accident reached me, a few weeks after the event, in a letter from my mother. I was living, as I said, in a bedsitter in Wandsworth, and I still had no telephone. I was not in regular contact with Beatrix at this time. Seeing her with the family was, I had found, too upsetting: upsetting for me, and disturbing for Thea, who for a good while remained much closer to me, and fonder of me, than she was of her mother. In these circumstances I had no choice, as far as I could see, but to back off, and keep my distance. So that is what I did. But of course, when I heard of the accident, I made contact with Beatrix immediately and visited her in hospital just a day or two later. She was just in the process of recovering from an initial operation on her neck which had, it transpired, gone quite seriously wrong. It was because of the failure of that operation, I seem to remember, that she had to return to hospital repeatedly over the next few years, often necessitating long absences from her family.

Poor Beatrix. She was no longer in pain when I went to see her, but her movement was very restricted. From then on she always carried herself stiffly – was never able to turn her head towards you, but always had to turn her whole body. She was told that it would be like that for the rest of her life. And then there was the seemingly endless hospitalization, which could not have come at a worse time. She had three children to look after – two of them very young. Charles was not much help, being very much absorbed in his work. He was a rather cold and unresponsive man, Charles, but thoroughly *decent* at heart, which I'm sure was to prove crucial over the next few years. I mean, Beatrix was hardly ever around, and there would have been great scope for him just bunking off back to Canada, or having an affair with the nanny or something, but he always did the right thing. He was straightforward and reliable. I'm tempted to say that these are essentially Canadian qualities, although perhaps you would consider that to be an absurd generalization. Anyway, his loyalty counted for a good deal, I know that. Where would the children have been without him, as their mother was shunted in and out of hospital for months at a time during their formative years?

And yet I would swear that it was his own son, and his own daughter, who received the lion's share of his attention. Who can blame him for that, in a way? Nobody. Certainly not me. But where did it leave Thea? Where did it leave your poor mother?

In this picture, Beatrix and I are not sitting close together. There is a good six inches of space between us, on what does not seem to be a very large bench. Perhaps I should not read too much into that. If either one of us is leaning away from the other, it is Beatrix herself. She is resting one hand on the arm of the bench and inclining herself towards it. I am leaning slightly forwards, if anything, towards the camera: I look ever so slightly impatient, as if I would quite like to get up and walk around in a moment. There is only so much that one can deduce from somebody's posture, but it would certainly be true to say that the nature of our friendship had changed, in the last few years. For some time, as you know, I had felt that I was tied to Beatrix by an unbreakable bond, a bond that went back to the time when I was evacuated to her home during the war. Well, I no longer felt that way. That notion had even started to seem a little childish to me; but it had been replaced by something else, something more real, and something which I believe was even more powerful. What drew me to

Beatrix now, what kept me loyal to her, was my love for her daughter. It felt to me (this might sound strange, I suppose) that Thea was in danger. I could not have said what kind of danger, although now I can see it quite clearly: she was in danger of not being loved, or not being loved enough. Saving her from this fate had become my secret responsibility. It would hardly be an exaggeration to say that it had taken on, for me, the nature of a sacred duty.

But then after all these years, Imogen, nothing seems quite so simple, quite so clear-cut. Was it really your mother who was starved of love, or was it me? If I felt an ache, a *yearning* to be in Thea's presence again, was that because, unselfishly, I wanted to help her, or because my own life was so empty and loveless? At this time I was working, by day, as a senior sales assistant at Arding and Hobbs department store at Clapham Junction; by night I returned to my little flat, cooked a cheap meal for myself, read trashy novels or listened to the wireless, and went to bed. I cannot pretend that it was anything other than a cheerless existence. I was making no real attempt to meet other people. I was not socializing with any of my work colleagues, or making any effort to appear friendly to them. Rebecca had been gone for more than four years, and I was still missing her terribly. (I still do, if you want to know the truth, although of course I have got used to the feeling, a long time ago.) The best way I can put it is to say that life had no flavour any more. Living without Rebecca was like living on an endless diet of bread and water. Somebody may have written that in a song once, it becomes so hard to remember what are your own ideas and what you may have picked up from somewhere else. Anyway, I must not start free associating again, and I must stop thinking about Rebecca; it is the story of me and Beatrix I am meant to be telling, me and Beatrix and how that all leads, inevitably, to you.

In the midst of all this, there was at least, for me, one bright spot: my elder sister, Sylvia, was married by now, to a man called Thomas. They had two children: a boy called David, and a girl called Gill. It is my niece Gill who, if all has gone according to plan, will deliver these tapes to you. They were just infants when this picture was taken but I do remember, round about this time, going up to the Midlands and spending a few days with my sister and brother-in-law, and liking it again, the experience of having small children around me. I would not say that I have been close to them as they have grown up, but I have watched over them, sometimes perhaps without their realizing it. That has been a source of consolation, I must say. Particularly over the last twenty years, after you and your mother disappeared from my life.

Just now, Imogen, a memory comes back to me. Something that happened not in the garden of the rest home, but in Beatrix's room. Was it on this same day, the day recorded on this photograph? Hard to be sure, since all of my visits followed much the same pattern. I would meet Beatrix downstairs, in the library or common room, and then we would take a walk in the garden and sit on this bench, or perhaps on one of the other benches, beside the little herb garden which was divided up into squares by miniature box hedges. After that, Beatrix would probably be tired, so I would take her back to her room and talk to her for a few more minutes while she lay down on the bed. There were pills that she was taking three or four times a day, and these often made her drowsy in the afternoons. Her window had Venetian blinds, I remember, rather than curtains. I would close these for her, but they did not close completely: thin strips of light and shadow would fall across her face and across the pale blue bedspread as she lay there, her eyelids gradually drooping. It's an image I remember distinctly. And one time – this time that I am telling you about – she had fallen asleep (or so I thought), and her breathing had become slow and regular, and I stood up and gathered up my things from her table and put on my coat and made my way to the door. Only, just as I got there and was reaching for the handle, I heard her slow, sleepy voice, saying: 'Ros?'

And I turned and saw that her eyes were still closed, even though her face and her body were turned stiffly towards me. I said, 'Yes, darling, what is it?' And then, very drowsily, she started mumbling. I found it hard to catch the words at first but they were more or less to this effect. She said: 'Why did he do it? Why did he just disappear like that?' I lifted my fingers from the doorhandle and took a few steps back towards her. My first thought was that she was talking about the lorry driver, but then I remembered that he had not disappeared, he had been arrested and given some trifling fine for careless driving. Then I wondered if she was talking about Jack, and the ending of their adventure in the gipsy caravan, but Jack had not so much disappeared as been driven away by her, so it wasn't him that she was thinking of, either. Nor was it Roger, the first husband from whom she was now divorced. 'Why?' she repeated. 'Why did he just run away?' And then I knew that in her half-sleep she was remembering Bonaparte, that foolish poodle of her mother's, and that cold winter's day, the day by the skating pond, the day he had run away over the horizon and disappeared for ever. 'I keep thinking about it,' she said. 'I can't stop thinking about it. It makes no sense. What had I done to him?' And I told her that she hadn't done anything to him, that sometimes things happened for no reason. I sat down on the bed beside her and clasped her icy hand, but nothing I said could console her, she began to cry, still without opening her eyes, a tear leaked out from beneath her eyelids and ran on to her cheek, and soon she was sobbing convulsively, uncontrollably, and I clasped her even more tightly and said more things to her, many more things that were meant to comfort her, but I can't remember what any of them were, and in any case she was somewhere else, by now, somewhere beyond comforting.

Shortly after this fourteenth picture was taken, my relations with Beatrix reached their lowest ebb.

I am not sure that you could guess that, however, from looking at the five smiling faces captured here. The year is 1962, and, my goodness, we look young in this picture, Bea and I! But then I realize, with a shock, that we *were* still young. I would have been twenty-nine, she would have been thirty-two; at which age, of course, the three-year difference between us, which seemed so momentous when we were both children, can have meant nothing at all. Twenty-nine, though! Is that all? A stripling, I would have been, an infant, and yet . . . and yet in my memory, the day this photograph was taken, I feel *ancient*. The reason can only be, I suppose, that a cycle was coming to an end; a circle was closing; the story of my friendship with Beatrix had not much further to run. That part of me which had been tied to her for so long was about to die.

Anyway, the important thing, as I must always remember, is that I describe the picture to you, that

I help you to see. So, let me focus my attention, once more.

Very well:

A beach hut, painted a rich blue, with the long grass of the sand dunes behind it. The thin strip of sky you can see at the back of the picture is several shades paler than the blue of the beach hut. The hut itself is a simple enough structure, just a wooden shed, really, with the two halves of the roof forming an apex at the top. Just beneath the apex, someone has painted the number of the hut, 304, and its name, 'Sasparella', which I think means the west wind or something.

The twin doors of the hut are flung open, and are painted white on the inside. They open to reveal a wide doorway, with a white lace curtain which has been pulled back and tied into place. Beyond the doorway, the interior of the hut is shadowy, but a few details can be made out. There is a small cupboard unit, also painted white, and on top of it, a little gas hob and a kettle. It is standing against the back wall of the hut, which is bisected diagonally by a large cross-beam. The interior of the hut is by no means large – about six feet square, I would guess. To the right there are three hooks on the back wall, one of them with a blue and yellow striped beach towel hanging from it. In the same corner, two children's fishing nets are leaning against the wall. There are some buckets and spades, I think, on the floor – a confusion of more blues, yellows and reds, anyway, although this part of the picture is really too shadowy to make out very much more.

On either side of the hut, you can just see the walls of its immediate neighbours. There is only about two feet of space between each hut. In front of the hut is a wooden platform, about the same area again as the hut's interior, and raised about one foot above the level of the beach. There is a windbreak set up on the left-hand side, patterned with wide blue, orange and yellow stripes. There are five people sitting on the platform: Beatrix and myself, to the rear, in deckchairs, and sitting to the front of the platform, with their legs dangling over the edge, her two youngest children, Joseph and Alice. Your mother, aged almost fourteen when this photograph was taken, is standing to the right of the others, positioning herself between the adults and the young children. Beatrix's husband, Charles, is not in the photograph, so I assume he must have taken it.

It is always possible, however, that Charles was simply not with us on the beach that day, and that we asked a stranger to take the photograph. The whole of that long summer, which Beatrix and her family spent down on the south coast, he only came down to see them at weekends. The rest of the time he remained in Pinner, and went to work every day in the City.

I went down to stay with the family for a fortnight, I remember. It was the same fortnight that the children's nanny had herself gone on holiday to visit her parents in Scotland. It turned out that it was very much in the capacity of her replacement that I had been invited.

Of course, I did not realize this at first. I assumed that Beatrix wanted my company. Perhaps my suspicions should have been aroused when I saw the room that I had been allocated. They had taken a short lease (two months or so) on a delightful house near Milford on Sea. It must have cost them a fortune, but then, I'm sure Charles was probably earning a fortune at that stage. It was enormous, with eight or nine bedrooms, a library, a games room and grounds extending to several acres, which included a formal rose garden and a private tennis court, all surrounded by woodland, giving them total seclusion and privacy. A more idyllic setting for a family holiday it is hard to imagine; and it came with the further benefit of the keys to this bathing hut, as I have described.

As for my room, it was at the very top of the house, in the attic. It was the kind of room you might have set aside for the scullery maid. Of course it was a privilege, and a pleasure, in my situation, to be spending any time in that house at all. I am not trying to imply that I was uncomfortable, or anything like that. I'm just saying that my status, from the very beginning, was made very clear to me.

I can't say that I ever warmed much to Beatrix's younger children. There was nothing *objectionable* about them – please don't assume that I am saying that – but at the same time, there was nothing exceptional about them, either, and I'm afraid that, perhaps through some insufficiency of my own, I have only ever enjoyed the company of exceptional children. I am not talking about IQs or early signs of musical genius: I'm talking about the way they look, the way they talk, their sense of humour, their sense of fun, a certain quality of animation and vitality which you find in some children and which makes you glad to be around them. Your mother had these qualities in abundance: I had discovered that much during those years, those very special years, when Rebecca and I had been lucky enough to have her living with us. Joseph and Alice, I'm afraid, did not. For one thing, they were plain, which is odd considering that they had two handsome parents. Joseph's complexion, as can be seen from this picture, was on the pale side – pale and blotchy, to be blunt about it – so that he tended to have a sickly look, as if always on the brink of ill-health. He looks *worried*, in this photograph, and this is how I remember him. He seemed to live life in a state of permanent, almost weepy anxiety, although it would most likely be provoked not by some great existential problem (some children, you know, can obsess over such things), but by more simple conundrums such as where his next treat was going to come from. He was despondent if somebody was not pampering him, fussing over him. From the look of abject misery on his face here, as he sits bare-chested in his navy-blue swimming trunks, shoulders hunched against the cold or perhaps just against the world in general, I would be prepared to wager that he had not had an ice cream for at least five minutes, and was not feeling at all happy about it. How old would he be, at this point? Almost seven, I should think, and Alice was a couple of years younger, so she would be five. She is prettier, by a small margin. Blonde hair, perfectly straight, almost shoulder length. She is wearing a red V-necked swimsuit, which is decorated at the tip of the 'V' with a single white flower like a daisy. She is gripping tightly on to the platform as if afraid of falling off, and looks vaguely cross about something but might just be squinting into the sunlight. Perhaps she has just had a quarrel with Joseph: they were always fighting, over the pettiest and most tiresome things – usually where to sit. They fought over where to sit at the dining table, at the cinema or at the circus, on the picnic rug or even at the back of the car. Endless, small-minded territorial disputes. You could understand the whole, sorry history of human warfare just by observing their behaviour for half an hour. It was very wearing.

Neither Beatrix nor I are wearing bathing suits, although it was a good summer, I remember, and we did swim off that beach, on several occasions. But today, it seems, was not one of those days. I have chosen a white, short-sleeved blouse, and a pair of beige khaki shorts which come almost to the knee. The ensemble is completed by sturdy leather sandals, open-toed, which reveal that I was not, unlike Beatrix, in the habit of painting my toenails. Hers are painted green, rather amazingly and inexplicably. She is barefoot and is wearing a floaty pale yellow and green summer dress, a sleeveless dress with a plunging neckline. Very glamorous, I must say. She would have turned heads wearing *that* as she walked down the main street of Milford on Sea! I look very dowdy by comparison. I think if I had cut my hair any shorter, at this stage, I might have been mistaken for a skinhead.

So, there we all are. The happy family, on holiday, minus the paterfamilias but with the useful addition of the loyal family friend. I almost said 'maiden aunt', because that's what I was starting to feel like. It would be a few more years, still, before I met Ruth; and meanwhile, as things stood, it has to be said that I'd been single for a *very* long time. Rebecca's departure, and my consequent loss of daily contact with Thea, had brought on a terrible sadness, which had long since settled on me and become a fixture. I had grown accustomed to living with this dull, insistent pain, which had a habit of flaring up, whenever I saw Thea, into something more deadly and piercing. To be readmitted into her presence was to be offered both joy and torture. Joy, for the obvious reasons; torture, because of the ever-present knowledge that this joy was to be temporary, short-lived. This summer I knew that I had just two weeks to enjoy her company. After that it would be back to London, work and loneliness.

I dare say that I was not the liveliest company, in these circumstances. But even if I was a rather gloomy presence in that household, at least there was a consistency to my mood, and children, on some level at least, appreciate that. Around me, around my melancholy, they could find stability. Beatrix on the other hand was volatile and unpredictable. She had always been like that, to a certain extent, but it seemed to me that her mood swings were now becoming extreme. Half of the time she behaved with a kind of desperate levity and high-spiritedness, but this could easily switch, without warning, into savagery. The dividing line between the two was very thin, although after a while I trained myself to observe when the change was coming. The mistake, I realized, was to leave her alone for more than a few minutes. The slightest opportunity for introspection meant that she would start brooding over her recent misfortunes, and soon afterwards a deadly bitterness would come over her. When this happened, nobody could escape her spite and rancour. Even Joseph and Alice were liable to find themselves being screamed at, usually for some minor domestic misdemeanour such as not picking their clothes up from the floor or spilling a drop or two of orange squash down the front of a shirt. Charles was not immune, either, and his daily telephone calls (he tended to phone most evenings, shortly after dinner) would often culminate in fearsome shouting matches during which I heard – as did the children – swear words, vile insults and obscenities which I didn't even understand, in many cases, and had certainly never come across before: not from female lips, at any rate. Poor Charles, needless to say, had done nothing to merit any of this abuse, but it had become Beatrix's firm conviction that he was having an affair, or perhaps even a series of affairs, while staying up in London without her. It was a most unlikely scenario, if you had ever met the man. Besides being devoted to his family, and a near-workaholic, he simply wasn't affair material. That was my opinion, in any case. But Beatrix had somehow got it fixed in her mind that he was paying regular visits to a woman who lived a few doors down their street. A neighbour and family friend of theirs. She had no evidence whatsoever, needless to say, and, whenever Charles was actually with her, the delusion (which is certainly the right word for it) would quickly be forgotten. But I came to recognize the moments when it was stealing over her: moments when she would be sitting alone in an armchair by the French windows, overlooking the garden, a cup of tea in her hands, staring into the middle distance with a kind of fixed intensity, unseeing, her thoughts roaming treacherously elsewhere. Such moments would invariably be followed by an eruption of some sort.

And by now I'm sure you can guess – can't you, Imogen? – who would bear the brunt of those eruptions. Your mother, of course. Your mother Thea.

As I said, she would scream and shout at her other two children, often for the most trifling misdeeds. With Thea, I am afraid to say, her behaviour could be considerably worse than that. Let me tell you about one episode in particular. The episode that brought a premature end to my visit, in fact.

It was early in the afternoon, about halfway through what was supposed to be the second week of my stay. Thea and I had been out for a walk together that morning, along the winding lanes which lay between the house and the sea. We had been picking blackberries. After collecting almost a full bowl, Thea came back to the house and displayed it proudly to her mother, who glanced up briefly and muttered something but basically didn't show much interest, even though she loved blackberries and it had really been to please her that we had spent so long picking them. Then, after lunch, I had gone outside to sit in a deckchair and read some more of my book, while Thea went to the kitchen to start making blackberry jam.

I should have mentioned that, only a few days earlier, Beatrix had gone shopping in Lymington and had returned with a new blouse for her elder daughter. It was a very nice, and very expensive, white muslin blouse. Rather a typical gift, coming from Beatrix: she didn't buy her children many clothes, but when she did, they were the very finest that money could buy, and were often almost too beautiful to wear. This blouse would probably have cost more than ten pounds – a huge sum, in those days – but of course, you could hardly expect Thea or any other child to appreciate that. To her it was just another item of clothing, albeit an extremely pretty one, and one which she was truly happy and grateful to have been given.

You can see what is coming next, I imagine.

Sure enough, Thea was wearing the blouse – still only a day or two old – that afternoon when she began making her jam. She was boiling up the blackberries in a big saucepan and she had the gas turned up too high, and the berries started to bubble and occasionally spit out of the pan, and soon she had quite a few blobs of blackberry juice splashed over the white blouse. She didn't even notice it herself, as far as I know, but her mother noticed it as soon as she came into the kitchen.

As I said, I was sitting outside reading at the time, so I could hear the gist of the conversation, if not all of it. 'What the *hell*,' Beatrix shouted, 'what the hell have you done to that effing blouse?' (I'm sorry, I cannot bring myself to repeat her words exactly.) Thea must have looked down at the blouse and gasped, and then things almost immediately got ugly. Ugly words, ugly deeds. Beatrix told her daughter that she was stupid, that she was the stupidest girl she had ever known. Thea burst into tears and said that she was sorry, so sorry, she would wash the blouse herself. Beatrix laughed and screamed at her that there was no point, the blouse was ruined now, and then she seized on this word and repeated it over and over, saying 'You've ruined it! The way that you ruin everything! Everything!' And the next thing that I knew she was accusing Thea – yes, I heard it with my own ears – of having ruined her health and ruined her life. 'It was all because of you!' she shouted. 'It's all your fault that I'm like this. The accident was all your fault. If it hadn't been *you* that I was picking up from school . . .' At which Thea screamed something inaudible, the words strangled by her tears, and ran from the kitchen, ran away up the stairs.

Her mother's voice (just like the voice of Ivy, when I had stood outside her bedroom door all those years ago and listened to her chastising Beatrix) was murderous. There is no other word for it. I could feel at once that there was violence in the air. Bea was beside herself, completely out of control.

I was shocked beyond words, but also paralysed by indecision. I wanted to reprove Beatrix for saying such horribly cruel and unjust things to her daughter, but this was not the right moment, while she was in such a frenzy. To know that I had overheard would probably enrage her even further. While I was outside dithering, in any case, I heard her yank open a drawer in the kitchen and then leave the room. Her footsteps pounded up the stairs, in pursuit of Thea, and she continued to shout at the top of her voice – wicked, unspeakable words. She said that Thea had brought her nothing but pain and trouble; that she wished her daughter had never been born. I ran into the house myself and got halfway up the stairs when I heard Thea's bedroom door slamming shut and being locked. Fortunately she could lock it from the inside; if she hadn't been able to do that, God knows what would have happened. I could see Beatrix running along the corridor towards the door then, and I could see that she had a carving knife in her hand. At once I called out to her to stop, but she didn't hear me. The next moment, thwarted by the locking of the door, she raised the knife and drove it into the door with tremendous force, again and again, scoring deep lines into the woodwork. All the time she was yelling at Thea to come out of there and calling her a little bitch and even worse names, names no mother should ever call her daughter. (Her fourteen-year-old daughter, for pity's sake!) Without pondering the consequences, for myself or anyone else, I ran towards her and seized her by the shoulders. I implored her to stop, and in a few seconds the knife had been dropped to the floor. Beatrix herself turned and stood with her back to the door, leaning against it, staring at me – or rather, *through* me. Her shoulders were heaving. She did not stay like that for long. Soon she pushed past me, hurried downstairs and left the house. Neither of us addressed any words to the other.

I think I need a few moments' rest, after telling you all that. Would you excuse me, Imogen, while I turn this machine off? I think I might be in need of a glass of water.

Yes. That is much better. Now I can resume.

Where was I? Outside your mother's bedroom, I believe.

I knocked on her door and asked if I could come in. She was distraught, and said nothing at first, just threw herself into my arms and stood there, crying. After a while I guided her towards the bed, and she lay down upon it. I lay beside her, and put my arms around her. We stayed like that, I remember, for some time, until Thea had calmed down and then fallen into an uneasy, exhausted sleep. Later on, when the sky clouded over, and the room grew chilly, I arose, fetched a spare blanket from the top of Thea's wardrobe, and draped it over us. After that, we were more comfortable.

In this way, the remainder of the afternoon slipped by. There was only one further incident worthy of mention. I opened my eyes, at one point, and noticed that the bedroom door was standing ajar. I had not heard it open. I glanced across and realized that Beatrix had returned to the house. She was staring at us. All I could see of her – or at least, all I can now remember – was her eyes: bloodshot, rounded, locked on to the recumbent figures of Thea and myself with a bulbous, mesmerized fixity. The image reminds me now, more than anything else, of the character Gollum from *The Lord of the Rings*, with his gaze and his thoughts concentrated on his 'precious'. I don't know why that comparison should occur to me, but it does: I hope it doesn't seem too grotesque or inappropriate.

Our eyes met, for the briefest of moments: Beatrix's and mine. Then she was gone, silently. I allowed my head to drop back against the pillow and was surprised to notice how fast and fiercely my heart was beating.

Slowly, as the evening progressed, the household returned to something like normality. I came downstairs and cooked supper for everyone, leaving Thea to slumber on for another hour or so. When she at last emerged from her bedroom and came down herself, the first thing she attempted to do was to hug her mother, who returned the gesture coldly and indifferently. I flashed Beatrix a reproving look, but it went unnoticed. She seemed to have cheered up considerably since the afternoon's upheavals. I wouldn't even say that her cheerfulness seemed forced or strained: she was in genuinely high spirits, and was even jollier when Charles phoned up to say that, earlier in the evening, he had locked himself out of the house and sprained his ankle trying to get in through an upstairs window. Beatrix thought this was hilarious, and for her youngest children she painted a most vivid word-picture of their father's discomfort and misadventures. All of which I listened to with a certain bafflement, I must say. Thea herself did not join in.

Finally the children were put to bed (by me), and the two of us were left alone together downstairs. The conversation which followed was one I have never forgotten.

I had never once, in my life, spoken a word of criticism of Beatrix to her face. I suppose I had always been too scared of her. Tonight, if anything, I was more scared of her than ever. Nevertheless, I could hardly hold my tongue, after the scene I had witnessed this afternoon. And so, after we had both been sitting in silence for a few minutes, as the shadows lengthened on the lawn outside, I first of all spoke her name very softly and then, once she had turned her head stiffly towards me, I said: 'I do think your behaviour towards Thea this afternoon calls for some explanation.' On hearing these words, she smiled at me – a brittle, challenging smile – and answered: 'How strange. I was going to say the very same thing to you.' I did not understand this remark, and I said so, adding: 'After all, I was not the one who attacked her with a knife.' 'I attacked her *door* with a knife,' Beatrix corrected me. 'There is a world of difference. I never laid a finger on Thea – nor would I, however much she provoked me.' 'You intended to harm her,' I said. To which she replied: 'What I intended is neither here nor there. I repeat: *I* never laid a finger on her.' There was such a strong emphasis on the personal pronoun that I immediately caught her drift – and, not for the first time that day, found myself astounded and horrified beyond words. 'Beatrix,' I cried, '*exactly* what are you implying?' She answered: 'You know very well. You know very well that I saw you, beneath the sheets, with my daughter.' And then, with quiet but careful emphasis, she added: '*Touching her.*' I sat there for a few seconds, open-mouthed, my mind reeling, before saying: 'Beatrix, what on *earth* do you mean?' She looked at me coolly and said: 'I know you, Rosamond. I know what you are. Don't think that

Thea has never told me: what you used to get up to, with *that woman*. When you were meant to be looking after her.' And, having delivered herself of these words, she picked up a magazine from a nearby table, and began to read.

I got up, left the room, and climbed the stairs to my bedroom, trembling with rage. The next morning, I packed my bags and returned to London.

That rage has never left me, Imogen. I feel it even now. I saw on that day – that evening – what a cruel and manipulative person Beatrix had become. Perhaps she had always been that way, and I had been unable to see it. Once again, in any case, she had succeeded in separating me from her daughter, at a time when Thea really needed me. That was a tragedy, for both of us, but I did not see that I had any choice. And I was still determined not to abandon her entirely, however hard Beatrix tried to make that happen. I would find ways, somehow or other. That was still my resolve.

I am tempted, now, to crumple this photograph up and throw it away. The smiles on our faces nauseate me. Well, the smile on my face, anyway; and hers. None of the children are smiling, in point of fact – Thea with better reason than most. What a deceitful thing a photograph is. They say that memory plays tricks on one. Not nearly as much as a photograph does, in my view. Let me put this lying image to one side, close my eyes, and think back to that day.

What do I see?

Clouds. White clouds, drifting against a pale grey

sky. The sky framed by the small latticed window in Thea's bedroom, at the back of that sad, beautiful house. I watch the patterns, the ceaselessly changing patterns, forming and dissolving, forming and dissolving, as the long afternoon slips away in near-silence. Sometimes a cry from the garden, the sound of the younger children, as they carry on with their game. Thea asleep beside me: so young, so vulnerable, so bewildered. The pressure of her body against my arm, and the cloud patterns forming and dissolving, forming and dissolving. White against grey, and the pressure of her body . . .

Number fifteen, and we are back to Warden Farm again. At long last! It's Christmas, now. The night before Christmas 1966. They adored Christmas, Ivy and Owen, and could never wait till the day itself to start celebrating. The first of many big meals always used to take place on Christmas Eve. Just look at us – the whole family sitting around the kitchen table. Eleven people, I can count. I wonder if I can put names to all the faces, after all these years.

Well now. There are my mother and father – that's easy enough. And Ivy and Owen, of course. So that's the older generation dealt with.

Only one of Ivy's sons is present: that must be Digby, who would already have been in his mid-thirties, and newly married to the tall, slightly toothy, rather giraffe-like woman sitting next to him. Her name, I think, was Marjorie, though I cannot be sure of that. The other son, Raymond, already had a wife and children of his own and must have been away with them somewhere. Beatrix and her family – most of her family, I should say – were in Canada. Sitting next to Marjorie is my sister, Sylvia, and next to her is an empty chair which should have been occupied by her husband, Thomas, my brother-in-law. Where is he, I wonder? Ah . . . taking the photograph, of course. How silly of me. I seem to have been sitting next to Thomas, and next to me, looking very sulky indeed in her yellow party hat (we are all wearing party hats), is Thea. Eighteen years old, she would have been. I shall tell you in a moment why she was there, all alone, without the rest of Bea's family, and I shall tell you why I was there, too, but first of all, to complete the picture, I should just mention the two small children who are sitting opposite each other at one end of the table. These children are David and Gill, my nephew and niece. She is about nine and he is about seven, at this time. (Gill, of course, is grown up now and, as I think I have told you already, she will be looking after my effects when I am gone.)

Meals at Warden Farm were nearly always taken in the kitchen, rather than the dining room. In that respect (as in many others) little had changed since the war. The dining room was dim, austere and forbidding. A chill seemed to hang over it; whereas the kitchen had always been one of my favourite haunts, during the time of my evacuation. Partly, I suppose, that had been down to the friendly, talkative presence of the cook. She was long gone, now: the days of Ivy and Owen's prosperity were fading, and they no longer employed any domestic staff. But it was impossible not to be cheered by the warmth and cosiness of that kitchen. I remember the colour of the flagstones, in particular, although you cannot see them in this picture: they were smooth and ruddy, the same reddish-brown colour as the mud that Uncle Owen would bring into the house on his Wellington boots after he had been out feeding the pigs. Everything in the kitchen seemed to be touched by this same reddish light; it bounced back off the copper ladles and saucepans which you can see hanging on the wall at the back of this photograph. The warmth of that kitchen was the warmth of a glowing hearth; the warmth at the crackling centre of a good log fire. It was a good place to be, on Christmas Eve. I was glad that I had chosen to come there, and glad, for all her obvious discontent, that I had persuaded Thea to come with me.

Christmas was always a problem, in those days. It is a difficult time for the single woman. Yes, Imogen, I was still alone, and still living in my bedsit in Wandsworth, although in other respects, life was starting to improve. I'd handed in my notice at the department store, taken courses in typing and short-hand, and found myself a job as secretary to the director of a publishing house with offices in Bedford Square. It was the beginning, did I but know it, of my career in publishing: my introduction to the circles in which I would, a few years later, meet my dear companion Ruth. However, that was still in the future.

In the meantime, I was not sanguine at the prospect

of another Christmas spent in spinsterly isolation. My father had retired, by now, and my parents had moved to Shropshire, to a large, very lovely cottage which lay only a mile or two from Warden Farm and indeed formed part of Uncle Owen's estate. It came with a substantial garden and three adjoining fields which were usually occupied, under some informal arrangement, by a pair of racehorses belonging to one of their neighbours. My sister and her husband visited regularly, and a tradition of spending Christmases there was soon established. David and Gill loved it, of course: loved everything about it. But only six people could sleep there, so I was left to make my own arrangements. There seemed to be an assumption that, because I lived alone in London, I must have been part of a wildly Bohemian circle of like-minded souls, and the idea of a conventional family Christmas in Shropshire would have horrified me. In fact it was exactly what I wanted.

This year, anyway, my mother hit upon the bright idea of asking Ivy if she could put me up at Warden Farm. She agreed – I don't know how readily – and I arranged to travel up by train on Christmas Eve.

Since the incident at Milford on Sea, my relations with Beatrix had, to put it mildly, been more difficult than ever; although the strange thing was that the difficulty appeared to be all on one side. *She* liked to pretend that nothing had happened. Just a few weeks later, she had telephoned and invited me out to dinner. I had been expecting her, at the very least,

to offer some sort of apology for her shocking behaviour; but instead, she chattered away all evening,
generally on the most trivial of subjects, apparently
quite oblivious to the terrible damage she had inflicted
upon her daughter, and upon my feelings, earlier that
summer. It was most peculiar; and I confess that, from
that point onwards, I was not just wary of Beatrix
(I had been that for some time) but actually found
it difficult to sustain a civil conversation with her. As
always, the force that kept drawing me back towards
her was Thea: my desire – you might almost call it a
need – to watch over her, to make sure that she was
not being entirely starved of love and attention. None
the less, Beatrix made it as difficult as possible for me
to fulfil this desire. Invitations over to the house in
Pinner were rare. If I tried to arrange a weekend out-
ing with her family – to Richmond Park, for example,
or Box Hill – it would often mysteriously turn out that
Thea could not come, having a prior engagement
with one of her friends. Beatrix did her level best, in
other words, to ensure that I saw her elder daughter
rarely, if ever at all.

It was late at night, the night before Christmas
Eve 1966, when the telephone rang in my flat, and I
heard Thea's voice on the line. She was eighteen years
old now, and was ringing to tell me that, following the
latest argument with her mother, it looked as if she
was going to be spending Christmas all alone. The rest
of the family had gone to visit Charles's parents in
Canada for three weeks. Thea had either refused to

go, or been forbidden from going – I never did quite establish the full details. What *was* clear was that she didn't relish the prospect of rattling around in a six-bedroom house in Pinner all by herself for the whole of the festive season. She asked if she could come over and stay with me, in my flat. When I told her that I wouldn't be there, because I was planning to spend Christmas with her grandparents – whom she had met perhaps two or three times in her life – she was at first nonplussed. And then I made the obvious suggestion: that she should come with me. I must say, I thought that the prospect would appeal to her; even excite her. Warden Farm was (to my mind, at least) such a thrilling and mysterious place, still, that I could not see how the opportunity of spending a few days there could seem anything other than tantalizing. But Thea betrayed no emotion at all when she agreed to catch the train with me the next day. Her voice was quite flat and toneless, and I have to admit that I was disappointed. I got far more of a reaction out of Ivy when I telephoned the next morning and informed her that I would be bringing her eldest granddaughter to stay with me over the Christmas period. I wouldn't say that she sounded pleased, but the news certainly seemed to affect her. 'Flabbergasted' might be the best way to describe her response.

We took the train to Shrewsbury the next day, Christmas Eve, and it was my father who picked us up from the station and drove us over to Warden Farm. The sky was silver-grey. A pale late-afternoon sun washed the meadows and hedgerows in winter light. In London there had been dustings of snow. Here it lay thick and deep: unbroken swathes of smooth, white velvet. I had not travelled these roads for ten years or more. They seemed utterly familiar; and at the same time, utterly strange and other-worldly. I could not reconcile these two feelings. I can remember this sensation – this thought – very clearly. The realization that sometimes, it is possible – even necessary – to entertain contradictory ideas; to accept the truth of two things that flatly contradict each other. I was only just beginning to understand this: only just beginning to acknowledge that this is one of the fundamental conditions of our existence. How old was I? I was thirty-three. So, yes: you could say that I was just starting to grow up.

As we came close to the farmhouse, I asked my father to take the longer way round, through the village, so that we approached it from the south. This way, we could stop about half a mile from the house and have a good view of it through the elder trees by the side of the road. So this is what we did. And there it stood, just as I remembered it: ancient, commanding, ivy-clad; rooted in the soil, and seeming to belong so organically to the surrounding landscape that it was easier to believe it had grown from some seed scattered two centuries ago, than that it had ever been designed or constructed. Today its roofs were snow-capped, as were the tops of the trees that surrounded it. The fields that lay before it were ploughed, now, and carpeted in snow that rose and fell in furrows of pure whiteness, like waves on an Arctic ocean.

We drove on, and entered the farmyard through the back gate. Hearing my father's car crunch its way across the ice-covered yard, Ivy came running to the back door to greet us. I was reminded, powerfully reminded, of my first arrival there, more than a quarter of a century ago. Once again I felt myself enfolded in her smoky, doggy embrace, and heard her stretch out the words, 'Hallo, my dear,' to an unprecedented length. Then she saw Thea, and gasped. She put a hand on her shoulder, keeping her at a distance, and looked her up and down, delight and amazement on her face. 'Is that my granddaughter?' she asked, disbelievingly, then seized her with incredible violence (Thea looked briefly stunned and also, if truth be told, ever so slightly bruised) and clasped her in a vicelike embrace. While she found herself being clutched in this way, Thea's face was towards me: I looked at her, searching, again, for signs of emotion – joy, affection, discomfort, *any* kind of *feeling*, in short – but I could see nothing. There was no light in her eyes, nothing behind them, no spirit animating her at all.

Deadness.

At least in this photograph there is some expression on her face, even if she just seems to be cross that she has been made to wear a party hat. These hats had come out of Christmas crackers, the remains of which can be seen here lying strewn across the kitchen table.

The debris of the meal is visible, too, or some of it: I can see traces of ham and cold turkey and celery, and the discarded jackets of baked potatoes. Aunt Ivy has not changed, noticeably, since the last time we saw her in a photograph (1948, at your grandmother's wedding, wasn't it?). Uncle Owen, on the other hand, seems to have doubled in size. He is holding the half-chewed leg of a turkey in his right hand, and his lips are purple – which means, I think, not that he is about to have some sort of seizure, but that he's been eating beetroot. David and Gill seem to be lost in some conversation of their own – not surprising, I suppose – and David's hat (a red one) has slid down over his eyes: it is far too big for him. My mother, I have to say, looks a little remote and preoccupied. Was this the Christmas when she'd just been doing her jury service? They gave her a rather grisly and distressing case to deal with, I seem to remember. But I honestly couldn't say whether that was this year, or another year altogether.

No doubt we played charades at some point – that was a long-standing family tradition, though a very tedious one, in my opinion – but my next clear memory of the evening comes much later. Some time between eleven-thirty and eleven-forty-five, everybody left for the parish church, to attend midnight communion. Even David and Gill, despite being so young – I recall that quite vividly. Aunt Ivy was due to read one of the lessons: a regular duty, on her part. She was much in demand for this purpose because even in ordinary conversation her voice could be heard as far as the Wrekin. The only people who didn't go were myself and Thea.

I have been an atheist all my life – since the age of about ten or eleven, at any rate. There was no question of my attending the service, but as for Thea, I had no idea whether she wanted to go or not. When the time came for everyone to leave, there was a confusion of boots and coats being pulled on, doors opening and slamming, cars being driven off into the night. I said goodbye to my parents, to Sylvia and Thomas, to David and Gill, knowing that after the service they would be returning directly to their cottage, and I wouldn't see them until tomorrow afternoon. When that was done, all fell silent, and I went back inside, snugly believing that I had Warden Farm to myself for an hour or so: an agreeable prospect, I must say. The house was overheated by now, and the air inside was heavy and close. I decided, first of all, to step outside for a few minutes' fresh air on the front lawn, beneath the stars of that lovely, crystalline night sky.

As soon as I stepped through the front door, however, I realized that Thea, too, had decided to stay behind. She was standing beneath the big old oak tree, leaning against its trunk and smoking a cigarette. Her back was to me, and to the house, and she was staring across the fields. There had been a fresh snowfall in the last few minutes. It was all but over now, but still a few flakes spiralled down from the branches of the tree, and rested a moment on her dark green overcoat before dissolving into nothingness. I approached her and when I touched her lightly on the shoulder, she turned sharply. She seemed to be alarmed that I had caught her smoking, but I told her that I didn't mind. She offered me a cigarette, but it was many years since I had given up smoking, and I had no wish to start again.

Up until this moment, Thea and I had had no real opportunity for conversation. The train to Shrewsbury had been busy, and a compartment full of complete strangers was hardly the right audience for the kind of confidences I was anticipating. Since then, we had hardly once been left alone: the Christmas festivities had begun soon after our arrival at the farmhouse. Tonight, I would be sleeping in my old room, in my old bed beneath the eaves, and Thea would be sleeping next to me, in the bed where her mother used to sleep. How strange that would feel! What unexpected patterns were beginning to emerge; what curious circles of experience were being described. Certainly, it would be easy enough to talk once we were in bed, but I could not bring myself to wait that long. Circumstance had kept me at a distance from Thea all day, and I was hungry for closeness.

I began by asking if she missed her family. This drew an immediate, short response from her – something between an exclamation and a laugh – after which, her face resumed its former blankness. 'Not really,' was all she would say. 'Anyway,' she added, 'it has to be better than last Christmas' – at which point she described to me how, the previous year, her mother and Charles had had a furious row on Christmas morning, following which Beatrix left the house – still wearing her dressing gown and pyjamas – drove off down the street and was not seen again for three days. 'The worst of it was,' Thea told me, 'Charles wouldn't let any of us open our presents until she came back, for fear of offending her. So they just sat there, under the tree. *Agony* for Alice and Joseph.' 'And for you,' I said, taking her by the arm.

We walked on, across the lawn, crunching fresh footprints into the virgin snow. Light spilled out of the house, from the windows of the billiard room and the two sitting rooms: golden, cheerful Christmas light. As we moved away from the house, down towards the sunken lawn and the ha-ha, this light faded, and we were left only with the silvery glow of the moon – barely in its first quarter – amplified and reflected by the white mirror of glittering snow. All was quiet, deathly quiet. I was reminded, once again, of what a magical and solemn place this was.

'Poor Beatrix ...' I began, but Thea interrupted me scornfully. 'Poor *Beatrix*?' she said. 'What about us? What about the people who have to live with her?' I replied, gently enough, that Beatrix probably still suffered a good deal of pain and discomfort as a result of her accident. To which Thea answered: 'And do you think that justifies the things she says to me? Telling me all the time how useless and stupid and ugly I am, how she wishes I'd never even been born? Calling me every name under the sun? Accusing me of being a lesbian?' I assumed that she was referring to the episode at the seaside, a few years ago, but seemingly this was not the only time that Thea's mother had made this wild allegation. 'She saw me once,' she said, her voice low, bitter, thick with held-back tears, 'walking with my friend Monica. We were walking down the street, back from school – arm in arm. She said it then, as well. She called us a pair of dykes. After that, she wouldn't allow Monica to come round to our house. My best friend. I was *fifteen*, for God's sake. I was only fifteen.' I didn't know what to say to this. What *could* I say? I must have murmured some well-worn, meaningless words of consolation. They seemed to have no impact at all on the stiff carapace of resentment Thea had wrapped around herself. 'The worst thing,' she continued, 'is having to listen to everyone *else* – everyone she knows – telling us what a wonderful person she is, and how lucky we are to have her as our mother.' I asked who she meant by 'everyone else', and Thea mentioned her mother's work colleagues. It was news to me that she worked at all. Apparently she had taken a job at the local hospital: first as a volunteer, then in some paid managerial capacity. She was immensely popular with the staff, according to Thea.

I took her arm again and squeezed it tightly. Another banal, inadequate gesture, which failed to elicit any response. I looked at the moonlit, snow-covered garden all around us, watched over tirelessly by the secretive house, so inscrutable, so full of memories, and I thought for the hundredth time what a strange, contradictory person Beatrix was. I wondered if it would help Thea in any way – not to forgive her mother, but at least to understand her, to learn something of who she was, where she came from – if I were to explain how we had met, Beatrix and I, how the story of our friendship began. (Much the same impulse, I suppose, as the one willing me to talk on and on into this microphone.) Perhaps if words – phrases – gestures – were not enough, then *narrative* was what Thea needed: perhaps the narrative of that night, that night twenty-five years ago when Beatrix led me such a merry, circular dance, might help to unpick the tangles of her mother's character? Might it even help me to do the same thing? – since, even after all this time, I was really no closer to understanding Beatrix than Thea herself was. I thought it an endeavour worth pursuing; so I began by asking, tentatively: 'Does your mother ever talk about this house? Did she ever tell you how we met, during the war, and how we became so close?' I had it in mind to lead Thea towards the edge of the garden and to find, if possible – even in this darkness – the hidden path that led towards the clearing and the caravan. But she forestalled me, completely and quite unexpectedly, by saying: 'Mother never talks about you.'

I must have looked wounded, and my silence (which lasted I don't know how long) must have impressed her; for she then repeated the word 'Never'; and looked at me in something like – could it be *triumph*? – before dropping her cigarette and grinding it, fizzing and hissing, into the snow with a twist of her foot.

Then she turned and walked back towards the house. Leaving me to stand alone in the garden – abashed, even humiliated by what she had told me – until the cold drove me, too, back indoors.

On Christmas afternoon, while most of the family were sleeping off the effects of yet more turkey and wine, I did make my way to the secret path again. Over the years it had become densely overgrown – I had to force my way through a brittle chaos of unyielding branches, pockets of snow falling around me as I went – but in the end I reached what had once been the clearing, and the caravan was still there, slightly to my surprise. The door was locked, and the windows were by now too dirty to see through, even after I had brushed the snow away with my gloved hand; but even the very outline of it, that peculiar teardrop shape, summoned up a host of uneasy memories. After a few minutes I turned, shaking a little, and pushed my way back through the trees. Afterwards, when I told Uncle Owen where I had been, he could hardly believe it; he'd thought that the caravan was long gone; he had truly forgotten its existence. Together, we spent a good while searching for the key, but it was nowhere to be found. He even volunteered to force the door open for me, or break a window; but I turned down these offers, chivalrous though they were. It seemed right to me, entirely right, that there could be no going back inside.

I'm not sure that I can put a very exact date on this one. What are we up to now – is it number sixteen? Five more to go, then. Thank goodness! I am growing tired of this story, and you must be exhausted, listening to me chatter on for hours on end. Can you bear with me for just a little longer, Imogen? It will be over now, all over, very soon. A relief all round, I am sure.

As I said, the precise date of this one escapes me. Late in the 1960s, I would think, or early in the 1970s. I am going by the hairstyles, as much as anything else. Joseph must be about fifteen in this picture, and his hair is almost down to his shoulders. The height of fashion at the time, I'm sure, although today it looks faintly ludicrous; like the collar on his shirt, which must be about four inches wide. It wasn't just a teenage thing, either: Charles himself doesn't look much better. What happened to everybody, at that time? How did we all suddenly lose our dress sense?

I must get a grip on myself. This isn't what you

need to hear. I haven't even told you where we are or what we are looking at. Well, we are in Saskatchewan, Canada. A town called Saskatoon, to be more precise. We are looking at Beatrix's house, and at four figures standing in the driveway: from left to right we have Charles, Joseph, Alice and Beatrix herself.

It is a very substantial weatherboard house, painted white. The photograph doesn't show the houses on either side, but one has the immediate impression of being in a well-to-do neighbourhood. Behind the figures, in the top right-hand corner of the picture, one catches a glimpse of what is obviously a big, comfortable, expensive saloon car. The garden, what we can see of it, is laid to lawn, with bushes of white and pink rhododendron visible at the edges. It is a day of blazing sunshine, and all four members of the family are squinting into the camera lens.

I wonder about this house. Lovely though it is, I can't believe that a house – any house – in Saskatoon would have been worth as much as their place in Pinner. I heard someone use the term 'downsizing' recently but I don't believe it would have been current in those days. Why did they sell up and move back to Canada? Did Charles make some bad decisions in the City, I wonder, and come a financial cropper? Perhaps not. Perhaps they were just drawn to the fresh air and the wide open spaces. I imagine that the lifestyle over there was quite agreeable.

There is something uniquely attractive about a weatherboard house. This one has four wooden steps leading up to a wide, good-sized porch. Above the porch is a covered balcony, surrounded by window-boxes planted with red dahlias. You would be able to walk out on to this balcony from one of the bedrooms: Charles's and Beatrix's, I imagine. Above the balcony, the house rises to another floor: there is a little sash window at the apex of the roof, in the centre, where there must have been an attic bedroom, probably for Alice. Or even for Thea, I suppose, because she lived there for a while at least. Going back to ground level, on the left-hand side there is a long verandah, running the entire depth of the house. I can see two chairs on the verandah – there are probably more, but they are out of view – and a little table covered with a gingham tablecloth. On the table there is a clear glass vase, containing a large arrangement of blue, yellow and deep violet flowers, and next to that, a big brown earthenware jug.

I have to say that I like this photograph. It comforts me. Of course, it's sad that Thea is not in it, although there is always the possibility that she was the one taking it. But I don't think so. She would have been in her early twenties, now, and although she moved over to Canada with the rest of them and even went to university in Calgary for a while, I don't think she ever completed her degree, and soon afterwards she came back to England, alone. It's sad, very sad, that she was expelled, in effect, from her own family. I must not dwell on that; or rather, I *shall* be dwelling on that, at some length I'm afraid, while telling you about the next two or three pictures. But, as far as this one is concerned, as I said, I find it comforting. Beatrix looks happy here. They all do, for that matter. I know that everybody smiles for photographs – that's one of the reasons you should never trust them – but this is what I call a *real* Beatrix smile. It looks as though someone has just told her the most wonderful joke and she has only just stopped throwing her head back and laughing at it. She even looks at ease in her clothes: a plain fawn blouse and pale blue jeans. She never would have worn anything like that in England, but it suits her. She has a nice little gold pendant around her neck, too. I wonder who gave her that.

I can remember one curious fact about her relocation to Canada. It was to do with the letter which presumably came with this photograph (which I'm sorry to say I can't seem to find any more). Beatrix wrote to me very infrequently – there were Christmas cards, of course, usually with a few lines of family news scribbled on the inside. But letters were rare. Anyway, what I remember most distinctly about this one was the signature at the bottom, or rather the name: 'Annie'. Not 'Beatrix', but 'Annie'. Mulling it over, I decided it was just an absent-minded slip (though rather a large one, I would have thought) and when I wrote back I addressed her as Beatrix, as usual. And then towards the end of that year I received a Christmas card which was signed 'Annie, Charles and the children'.

Well, it was her prerogative to change her name,

I suppose, and it seems that from the moment she set foot on Canadian soil she dropped 'Beatrix' and never allowed anybody to call her that again, not even her husband or children. She had chosen to reinvent herself; to distance herself completely from the past.

One of the things she associated with 'the past', of course, was her first daughter.

I have nothing more to say about this photograph, really; but perhaps I should add something here, by way of postscript. This is the last picture of Beatrix that I possess, and because the rest of this story does not concern her directly, this might be the best time to tell you what became of her. What little I know, anyway.

Very well: about seven or eight years ago, when I was doing some shopping at the market in Shrewsbury, I ran into Raymond, her eldest brother. He would have been about seventy years old: he was enormously tall, and was wearing a three-piece suit which appeared to date back to the 1940s, and he had bushy side-whiskers and a moustache. In looks and manner and bearing he seemed almost grotesque – the relic of an era long disappeared, long forgotten by all but a few. You could see that he belonged to the countryside – had belonged there all his life – and felt completely out of place in the town. He looked for all the world like one of the extras on the set of *Gone To Earth*! Anyway, that is all by the by. He didn't recognize me, of course, and in a way I'm amazed that I managed to recognize *him*. We talked for only a few minutes, just enough time to catch up on each other's histories in sketchy detail. I was very selective about what I told him, as you can imagine. Towards the end of our conversation I asked him – with some trepidation – if he was still in contact with Beatrix. He told me that she had died, in 1991, at the age of sixty-one. A cancer of the throat, apparently. She had still been living in Canada, although she had separated from Charles. (I had long thought that was inevitable, given her paranoia about his non-existent infidelities.) In the last twenty years of her life she had resumed her career – very successfully, by the sound of it – in hospital management. Raymond told me that she'd ended up working at a small clinic in Alberta, where she was considered by the staff to be the best – and best-loved – manager they'd ever had. He said that they had been devastated when she died, and that her birthday was still marked there every year. One of the doctors had traced Raymond's address in Shropshire and one year, during a visit to England, had called on him to hand over a box containing some of his late sister's effects. It included a letter signed by all of the nursing staff, describing Beatrix as 'the nicest lady we have ever met' and 'a saint'. They admired, in particular, the way she had continued to live life to the full, even after sustaining such a terrible injury when she was young.

And so, Beatrix ... that is the end of your story. Beatrix, my cousin, my blood-sister. Very soon, perhaps, you and I will be in the same place again. But

I'm not sure that I want to meet you there. Will you recognize me, even if I do? And how am I supposed to address you, nowadays – as 'Beatrix', still, or 'Annie'?

Seventeen. Caravans again. More caravans. I told you that they would be back, before we were finished.

This is bleak, this picture. A chill comes over me when I look at it. It was an insufferably cold day, apart from anything else. The winter of 1975, somewhere on the Lincolnshire coast. An icy wind blowing in off the North Sea.

There are four caravans (or should I call them mobile homes?) arranged in a sort of crescent around a patch of grass. You can only see the front of these big, squat, ugly things in this photograph. The grass itself is scrawny and muddy, and dusted white with traces of snow or ice. Off the edge of the picture you would find more mobile homes, and then still more, and still more, stretching away into the distance. There were probably a hundred or more on that particular site. I sometimes wondered how it was possible to be sure of finding the right one. More than once, apparently, Martin had got lost trying to get home on his way back from a drinking session.

Now I'm getting ahead of myself again. You do

not even know who Martin is, yet. Well, he was Thea's partner. Not husband – I don't believe they were ever married – but her partner, and the father of her child. Which of course makes him your father, Imogen.

Bearing that in mind, I shall try to be kind about him, although I must say that I didn't take to him at all, on the one occasion that we met. The occasion of this photograph, that is.

Well, here they both are, anyway, standing in front of the mobile home. Here *you* are, I should say – all three of you – because, yes, you are in this photograph too, Imogen! At long last. You are born! I bet you were beginning to think that we would never get there. You are only a few months old, however, at this stage, and all that can really be seen of you is your tiny face peeping out from the white blanket in which Thea has swaddled you. As I believe I said earlier, on another tape – days and days ago, it seems – all baby faces are much the same. So let's take a good look at the faces of your parents instead.

Martin. Well. He was a little younger than your mother, I seem to remember. Probably about twenty-two, when this picture was taken. Too young to be a father. Much too young. He has dark brown shoulder-length hair, and a droopy moustache. Black leather jacket, T-shirt and jeans. The jacket has another of those terrible 1970s wide collars. He is very pale, with a prominent windpipe and Adam's apple, and bad skin. His T-shirt has a picture of Adolf Hitler on the front, and underneath it the caption 'European Tour, 1939–1945'. I seem to remember that he thought this very amusing. Thea told me that she'd had complaints about this T-shirt from other people on the caravan site: there were a lot of older people living there, including some veterans of the war. She did not seem to take these complaints very seriously. Her relations with the neighbours were not good.

From what I can see of your mother's clothes – I can't see much of them, because of the way she is holding you – she appears to be wearing a leather jerkin or waistcoat, over a white polo-neck shirt, which comes high up under her chin. Her hair is long and centre-parted. Leather sandals, open-toed, over bare feet, which I would not have thought was very practical, in that sort of weather. But I imagine that we were all outside for only a short time. Just long enough to take the photograph, and get back inside to the warmth.

And yes, it *was* warm inside that caravan, amazingly. They even had radiators in there, unless my memory is deceiving me, and a gas fire, and an electric bar fire too. You needed everything you could get, to fight against that dreadful North Sea wind. They were in a very exposed spot. But inside, it was almost cosy – except for the terrible chaos and untidiness. There was a good-sized sitting area, and a little open-plan kitchen next to it. Two tiny bedrooms – I mean *really* tiny, with no real floor space at all – and a tiny bathroom and a tiny toilet. The kind of place you might just about put up with, if you were only there for a few days, with someone you really liked, someone you didn't mind being close to. As a place to bring up a small child, with a man who was practically a stranger . . . Well, I don't think it was very suitable, to be honest.

A few weeks earlier Beatrix had sent me one of her very infrequent letters and in it she had told me the rather shocking news that she was now a grandmother. A grandmother, at the age of forty-five! She didn't sound terribly pleased about it, I have to say. I wasn't very pleased, either. I had seen almost nothing of Thea in the last few years. I knew that she was back in the country, but that was about all. My letters to her usually remained unanswered; one or two of them came back stamped 'Not known at this address', giving me to understand that she had adopted a rather peripatetic lifestyle. I was aware that, through one of her old schoolfriends, she had drifted into a sort of alternative circle, and had been living in squats with rock musicians and all that sort of thing. There was nothing I could do about this, and besides, it all seemed reasonably harmless. She certainly had no interest in taking any advice from me; that was made perfectly clear, more than once. As far as I knew, she had very few memories of the years she'd lived with Rebecca and myself in Putney. She did not regard me in the light of a surrogate mother – which was probably, at heart, how I wanted to be regarded; instead she appeared to think of me – if at all

– simply as a sort of troublesome and interfering maiden aunt, best avoided if possible. So be it. As I say, there was nothing much I could do. In other areas of my life I was much more . . . well, 'happy' is perhaps not the right word – *'fulfilled'*, at any rate – than I had been for some years. At the publishing house, I had risen from the rank of lowly secretary to senior editor: an important position. And I had met a very nice woman – and an excellent painter – called Ruth, and we had developed a great fondness for each other, and moved into a little house in Kentish Town. We led a busy and interesting life. It was all very satisfactory, on one level.

It was publishing business that had taken me to the North of England, I remember. I had been visiting one of our authors, a writer of historical romances, who lived in Hull, and whose latest offering presented some minor editorial challenges. A few glaring anachronisms, characters whose names kept changing from one chapter to another, that sort of thing. I spent two days at her home, going through the manuscript, and then, on the way back to London, I had arranged to call on Thea at this latest peculiar address I had been given by her mother: somewhere on the east coast. It would be the first time I'd seen her for at least two years.

I did not realize that she lived on a caravan park, and it proved to be a hellishly inaccessible place. I had to take the train to a town called Market Rasen, followed by a taxi journey of almost an hour. I arrived much later than I had promised, but neither Thea nor her boyfriend seemed particularly concerned. I got the impression that they had hardly been keeping an anxious look-out for me.

I disembarked from the taxi, and called at the site office to get directions to the caravan. I had with me a bunch of flowers, for Thea, and a small blue teddy bear, for you. I wonder what became of that bear. I suspect that it disappeared, into the chaos in which your mother and Martin lived. There was not just the usual domestic clutter you would expect from a couple with a young child – unwashed crockery, clothes hanging up to dry, and so on – but a good deal of musical equipment: electric guitars, instrument flight cases, even speaker cabinets. A ridiculous amount of gear, to keep in what was already a confined space. Martin called himself a musician, and indeed he treated me, at one point, to a rendition of some of his songs on the guitar, but I could see that he had little talent. Ruth's brother worked in the music business, and through him, later on, I came to appreciate the very high standard of musicianship that is required to perform even the simplest pop songs with anything like proficiency. Martin did not possess this skill. He did not make his living by performing music, in any case. By profession he was a roadie – I believe that is the term – for a pop group who were scoring some modest success in the singles chart around this time. Thea had met him after one of their concerts. I imagine it was one of the group members she had been hoping to meet, but they were all otherwise engaged, and perhaps Martin seemed, at the time, to be the next best thing. I am sorry, these details will probably be rather upsetting for you. This group was based in Sheffield and he spent a good deal of time there, away from Thea and his daughter, even when he wasn't touring, which in itself was at least half of the year. As you can imagine, she ended up seeing very little of him. And that was before he left her altogether.

How difficult it is to tell you all these things in the right order. As usual, I am supposed to be describing a photograph, and everything has gone higgledy-piggledy. But perhaps there isn't a right order, anyway. Perhaps chaos and randomness are the natural order of things. I sometimes think so.

Back to the photograph, then. But I can think of nothing more to say about it. A windswept caravan park in the north-east of England, a small baby and a couple who clearly had no long-term future together. What else could there be to tell you?

Two things struck me about Thea, during that visit. One was her complete and unconditional devotion to Martin, a devotion which was in no way reciprocated. I can remember the way she clung to him at every opportunity, the way she pampered him and poured his beer and brewed his tea – even, sometimes, when you, Imogen, were the one lying on your back in your cot and screaming for attention. The only time I heard her speak about anything with real passion and animation was later in the evening, after he had gone out to the pub and left us alone together, when she told me what a fine musician he was and how his songs were going to make them both a fortune some day. This faith was touching, but entirely misplaced, as far as I could see. The other thing I remember was her shocking temper. I first noticed it (again, after Martin had gone out – she seemed to be altogether calmer and more settled when he was around) when she was standing over by the stove, boiling up some water in a saucepan. It was the kind of pan where the handle itself gets hot, and she forgot to wrap a cloth around it when she was lifting it from the hob, and although she did not burn her hand badly it gave her a nasty shock. She dropped the pan with a scream and the water went all over the floor; she then yelled out a string of obscenities, and with all the strength she could muster she kicked the saucepan across the floor, then picked up a tea cup (which was still half full of tea) and threw it against the wall so that it shattered. Only then was she calm enough to run some cold water over her hands from the tap, and start helping me to clear up the mess. When you began crying, distressed by the sounds of your mother's anger, I was the one who picked you up and comforted you, when it became clear that she was not going to do so.

I ended up staying the night with you all, although that had never been my intention. Martin had promised to drive me to Market Rasen in time for the last train at about ten o'clock. However, he did not return from the pub in time. When there was still no sign of him, and it was getting on for midnight, Thea and I both went to bed. I squeezed myself into the smaller of the two minute bedrooms, and slept fitfully for a while. When I heard Martin get back, I glanced at my watch, and saw that it was three o'clock in the morning. He made a great deal of noise coming into the caravan, then got some food for himself and started playing his guitar, with the amplifier turned up loud. After a few minutes of this, he opened the door to the bedroom where you and Thea were sleeping. I could hear voices. Thea's voice was sleepy at first, then wakeful. Soon I heard the sound of Thea carrying you, in your carrycot, out into the caravan's living area, and leaving you there. She went back into her bedroom and then I heard your mother and father make love for a while. Then there was silence. Then you started crying. I lay in the dark, waiting for one or other of your parents to go and comfort you, but they didn't. After a while I got up myself, fetched you a bottle of formula milk from the fridge, and fed it to you. Gradually, you settled back into sleep. I sat there for two or three hours, watching dawn break over the caravan site, over the distant North Sea, while you continued to sleep in my arms.

That pale, forlorn winter sun had been struggling to break through the clouds for almost an hour when you finally woke up again. This time you did not cry out, or scream to be fed. You lay there, quite placid, and stared at my face, your eyes wide open and deep blue: cerulean blue, the colour of the sky over Lac Chambon . . . Yes, that same colour . . . It was as if you were trying to take in every detail of my features, commit them permanently to your infant memory. You still had excellent vision in those days, Imogen, as you doubtless know.

Here we are, then. Number eighteen. I have been putting it off – putting it off for days, now, telling you about this one. But it cannot wait any longer. The time has come.

And then, after this, there will be just two more pictures. We are near the end. And I am near to my end, too, Imogen: very near. Just an hour or so now, I should think. And then it will all be over. Just an hour! Not much, is it, when I think of the thousands, the hundreds of thousands of hours I have lived through. But there is nothing to be done about that. I am quite calm, now, and quite prepared. The only important thing, at this stage, is that I do my duty: that I repay what is owed to you. Which means describing this picture, and telling you, as best I can, the dreadful story that lies behind it.

Very well. This is your mother again. It is the last picture I have ever seen of your mother, in fact. I don't know when or where it was taken. It is in black-and-white, even though we are, of course, well into the era of colour photography. I clipped it out of a newspaper, and the reproduction was poor to begin with. Now the ink has started to fade, and the paper has started to curl, and it is harder than ever to make out your mother's features. No matter. This picture is all that we have.

It is really impossible to say, but I would *guess* that she was twenty-seven or twenty-eight when this photograph was taken. It is not a good picture of her face: her eyes are averted and she is looking both downwards and away from the camera, to the right of the frame. Her eyelids are half-closed. She is wearing (so far as I can see – it is all terribly hard to make out) a voluminous Afghan coat. And yet she is clearly indoors: you can see some sort of patterned flock wallpaper in the background. Her hair is full bodied, shoulder-length and parted slightly to the left, showing off her high forehead. A long strand of it hangs over her right eye. Her nose, in this picture, looks long and thin, which I must say is not how I remember it, but there you are: these things can be deceptive. Her expression ...? Well, that is not easy to describe, either. Would it be too evasive of me, if I were just to say 'inscrutable'? She is half-smiling: as if keeping some private joke to herself, withholding it from us, and from the camera. That is really all I can say. As I mentioned before, it is not a good photograph, and the newspaper's motive in publishing it, needless to say, was not to offer its readers any insight into Thea's character, but merely to enable them to identify her.

In that respect I'm sure that it served its purpose well enough.

Oh dear. This is so very difficult. For the first time (perhaps you will laugh to hear me say this) – for the first time since I began describing these photographs to you, I find myself lost for words. Or, to use a common expression in its most literal sense, *words fail me*. However difficult it has been, over the last few days, matching words to images, trying to find the words which will help you to imagine colours, shapes, buildings, landscapes, bodies, faces – however hard that has been, I don't believe that words have actually *failed* me, before now. But at last I find myself having to tell you the most difficult thing of all, and I simply don't know where to begin.

Let me turn this machine off for a moment, and allow myself a little while to reflect.

All right. This cannot be said easily, or kindly, so I shall just say it. It was your mother, Imogen. Have you guessed that by now? I dare say you have. It was your mother who blinded you.

I would like to say that it was an accident, but that was not the doctors' judgment; nor was it the judgment of the court, in the end. She lost her temper with you – I don't know what you had done, something very minor I am sure – and she struck you, and she shook you; shook you so violently that, since that day, you have not been able to see a thing. You were just a little more than three years old.

Do you remember, I wonder? Do you remember that happening? They told me that you didn't, that you had blanked it out. That you remembered other things, things that happened to you before then; but that day, that morning, that . . . attack – no. You had wiped it from memory. 'The mind has fuses,' as somebody once said.

Perhaps you should turn off this tape yourself, for a minute or two. You might want some time to think about these things.

In the meantime, I shall continue, anyway. I would quite like to get this over with.

It was Beatrix who told me, by telephone, a week or two after it happened. She had flown back from Canada as soon as she heard, and paid what I believe must have been a brief visit to her daughter. She was still in London when she telephoned me, although we did not see each other, on that occasion. 'Ros,' she said, 'it's Annie here.' Always Annie, by then. Never Beatrix. She had even begun to develop – or affect – a Canadian accent. She did not tell me much, only that Thea had been (these were *her* words) clumsy and stupid again, and that there had been a nasty accident. Her tone was, if not offhand, then certainly a little on the matter-of-fact side. She did not mention the seriousness of the damage to your eyesight. I found that out later. As a result I did not really take in the horror of what had happened, at all, until she told me where your mother was. In prison. A women's prison in Durham. The court had refused her bail, apparently, and she was there on remand, awaiting trial. I told Beatrix that I would go up there at once.

It was a difficult time. A horrible time. The prison was a ghastly place, much worse than anyone could have imagined. Your mother looked ... Well, once again, words are inadequate. Pointless. She was in a state of shock, of course. She was obviously incapable, at this stage, of taking in the enormity of what she had done. That blankness, that lack of response, which I had noticed during our Christmas at Warden Farm (twelve years ago! – twelve years, already) was ingrained upon her now. Her eyes were cold and lifeless, the eyes of someone who could no longer afford the risk of looking upon the world. It was impossible to tell whether she was pleased to see me or not. She hardly spoke to me, as I recall. I tried to extract the barest details from her, about what had happened on that terrible morning, but it was a hopeless task.

Martin had gone – I had guessed that much. Long gone, leaving you and your mother alone. Not on the caravan site any more, but in a little house, part of a new council estate somewhere near Leeds, I think. I don't know where he went, and I don't know what became of him. Frankly, it is of no interest to me, although I did notice that the only time Thea showed any sign of animation – any sign of *life* during that first visit – was when she implored me to try to find him, and bring him back to her. The poor, deluded thing. It seemed far more important, to me, that we should concentrate our efforts on securing the best possible future for you, Imogen; but that subject (it is dreadful that I should have to tell you this) barely seemed to interest her. That should give you an indication, at least, of what sort of place her recent experiences had brought her to. A place where her maternal feelings could not survive, could only wither and die; and not just her maternal feelings, but *all* feeling, except for this vacuous, affectless obsession with Martin. Martin who could not have cared less about her.

Well, in any case, *I* was the one who had been deluding myself, if I had thought that Thea and I were going to have any say in your future. As soon as you came out of hospital, you were put into the care of foster parents. That was a temporary arrangement, pending your mother's trial. She was held in prison for almost six months before the case came up. She was found guilty of causing grievous bodily harm – without intent, thankfully (that would have meant a much longer sentence) – and then sent back to prison for another six months. In the meantime, social services had the task of finding another family who were prepared to adopt you permanently.

In my opinion, the best and simplest solution was staring us all in the face: you would come down to London, to live with me and Ruth. We had a large, comfortable home. Neither of us had any other family commitments. And – from an entirely selfish point of view (grotesquely selfish, you might think now, considering what had recently happened) – it would light up the whole house, to have a young child living there. As I have said before, many times, I was enormously fond of Ruth. But it would not be true to say that she had filled, entirely, the emotional void in my life which had opened up after the loss of Rebecca. Whether she herself could sense this, I was not aware. I had never told her anything about Rebecca, in any case. And Ruth and I were happy with each other, and comfortable around each other, I am not denying that at all. But the thought of having you, Imogen, joining us, living with us, coming to love and depend upon us (and how much you *would* depend upon us, now that you had been so cruelly incapacitated) – it was almost too wonderful to contemplate. Nothing could ever compensate for the loss of your sight; nothing could undo the tragedy in which you and your mother had become embroiled. But *something* good might come out of this: I was determined. We would take you under our wing and give you, despite everything, a marvellous childhood: the best, most loving, most nurturing childhood anyone could wish for. We would give you everything your mother had never had. And in this way, perhaps, across the generations, the scales of justice might somehow be balanced. That, at any rate, was how *I* had come to construe the possibilities of the situation.

Ha! Well, I was mistaken. Sadly, sadly mistaken. And it wasn't Ruth who thwarted my plans, as you might have expected. Oh, she was reluctant enough at first. She took some persuading: and indeed, while I was persuading her, I could not help remembering all the similar conversations I'd had with Rebecca, more than two decades earlier, on the eve of her graduation day. That crisis had seemed serious enough at the time; now it appeared almost comically trivial. What tiny children we had been! How little I had foreseen of all the strange twists of fortune that lay ahead of me, far in the future! If only I had known, then, what would happen to Thea, what she would become ... But there is nothing to be gained – nothing – by going down that road. Turn back, Rosamond. Turn back at once.

No, it was not Ruth who stood in my way. The bureaucrats at social services were having none of it. It seemed that we were not suitable candidates for adoption, in this case. They sent us a cursory letter, in which it was stated that my own family ties with Imogen's mother were too close. That was the reason they gave. And who knows? Perhaps they were right after all. Yes, I suppose I can entertain that idea now. But at the time I thought it a feeble excuse. And dishonest. What they really objected to (this was my suspicion) was our situation in life: two ladies who had chosen to live together, and made no secret of the nature of their relationship. I had come up against this prejudice – subtle, unspoken, but unmistakeably *there* – time and again over the years. Outside the rather progressive and liberal circles in which Ruth and I moved, we were under no illusions as to how the rest of the world regarded us. We had grown used to being considered deviants and pariahs.

Anyway, I was not prepared to let the matter rest there. After your mother's conviction, when she had begun her sentence proper, I went to visit her again. It was the last time I ever visited her in prison; and on my way home, I had arranged to have an interview with my correspondent from social services. I had thought that, by meeting her face to face, it might be possible to break through her wall of obdurate officialdom. Which, to a degree – a very limited degree – I succeeded in doing. Certainly we had a civilized and, at times, almost cordial discussion. But I could not get her to understand my point of view. 'What puzzles me,' she kept saying, 'is that you have only ever seen Imogen once, by your own account. And yet you seem to be trying to persuade me that there is some extraordinary bond between you, which mustn't be broken.' What was I supposed to say to that? Imogen, it has taken me hours and hours, and probably tens of thousands of words spilled out on to this tape, to explain to you how that bond came to be forged. How could I be expected to do the same thing, in the space of twenty minutes, for the benefit of this well-meaning but essentially small-minded officer of the welfare state? It was hopeless. And besides, I was already too late. 'We have found a family for Imogen,' she announced with a smile I can only describe as triumphant. 'A lovely family.' I sat there, open-mouthed, gaping like a fish and doubtless looking extremely foolish. It was the last thing I had expected to hear. All I could find it in me to say, once the reality of the situation had sunk in, was: 'Am I to have no contact with Imogen, then? Is her mother to have no contact?' She replied that this decision lay entirely in the hands of the adopting family. I asked for the family's name. She refused to give it to me. This was intolerable – and I told her so, in no uncertain terms. It made no difference. She offered only one concession. 'You may write to them, if you wish, care of this office. You may write to them requesting contact. Our advice, to them, would be that such contact is rarely desirable. Imogen's relationship with her mother has been destroyed, damaged beyond repair. In these cases, a clean break is usually the most practical option; and also the kindest, for the child. Remember,' she said – fixing me with a penetrating glare, for some reason – 'that the interests of the child are paramount. Her interests, not those of the adults involved.'

I left her office in a cold rage; and sat for some minutes in my car, weeping with frustration, before beginning the long drive south to London.

Time to turn off the tape again. I'm sorry. I thought I had more self-control than this.

That's better. I have a glass of whisky by my side now. And a whole bottle next to it, almost full.

Bowmore, it is, an Islay malt, nice and peaty. It will come in very handy, I am sure, in the short time that is left to me now.

While I was in the kitchen just now, fetching myself this drink, I had a good think about what I've just told you, and it became clear to me – for the very first time – how foolish I still was in those days. Everybody – your new family, the social services people, even Ruth – everybody except *me*, in short – could see what was best for you. The odds against you were stacked so heavily now – you had so much to learn – a whole new way of perceiving and relating to the world – and in order to achieve that you needed love and care and *stability* above all. All of these things suggested that it would be far, far better to keep you well away from your mother from now on. That makes perfect sense, doesn't it? But I couldn't accept it. Even in my mid-forties, I still had this callow, overly benign view of the world. I still believed that reconciliation was possible; and more than that, how flattering it was, to my own self-esteem, to suppose that *I* could be the person to bring it about! I conceived of myself as this secretive, self-effacing, benevolent agency, plotting behind the scenes in order to engineer climactic reunions and miraculous healings of wounds. I couldn't quite see, yet, how it was to be done. But I knew that above all, my task called for two special qualities: patience, and cunning.

I kept in contact with your mother when she came out of prison. I do not like to think of the things she must have endured there, during those few months. Prisoners live by their own rules, and those who are known to have abused children are not treated kindly. Thea suffered badly, of that I have no doubt. Now that she was free again, we kept up an occasional correspondence, but I could not help noticing that she was reluctant to see me in person. And there had been another, unexpected development. There was a new man in her life: a Mr Ramsey, who had begun writing to her in prison – letters of a moral, religious and in my view sinister character. Thea was vulnerable, at this time, dreadfully vulnerable, and I had no doubt that this nasty, predatory person (who had apparently read of her case in the newspaper) was bent on gaining control over her, using for his purposes some distorted version of the Christian ideas of redemption and forgiveness, ideas that someone in her situation might well find almost irresistible. Towards the end of her sentence he had begun to visit her; and now, it seemed, they were to set up home together. I did not like the sound of it at all, but of course there was nothing I could do.

Meanwhile, I had devised a plan. Some intuition told me that it would be ineffective to write to your new family and ask them, straight out, if I might be allowed to see you. A less direct approach was called for. Instead, I wrote them a letter, outlining my relationship to you, and sketching the history of my long involvement with Thea and her family. I told them that I understood, very well, how desirable it was that you should now sever all links with your unfortunate past, and be given a completely fresh start; but said that you were, at the same time, still very much missed by some of your relatives. And in the light of that, I wrote with a simple, forthright request: might we be allowed to have a memento? Might it be possible, in fact, to have your portrait painted? A picture, it seemed to me, in which the artist had captured the very essence of you, the 'new' you, as you embarked upon your second, more difficult but more hopeful life – this would be a marvellously consoling thing to have. It would be something very much more significant than a mere photograph or souvenir, gathering dust on some wall or mantelpiece. A good portrait, after all, has an intrinsic vitality of its own: it is living, and organic. And what was more, I knew the very person to paint it.

And here it is. Picture number nineteen. Ruth's portrait of you, which she simply entitled 'Imogen, 1980'. I have it now, resting upon my knee. Unframed, oil on canvas, probably measuring about ten by fourteen inches. It was never framed, so far as I remember. Ruth herself did not think very highly of it, and for many years it was kept hidden away at the top of our house, in the room where she stored all of her abandoned canvases. A cold, dead, unvisited place, it was. She used to call it 'the failure room'. But it is a fine picture, in my opinion. One of her best. Her reason for disliking it had nothing to do with the quality of the picture itself.

It is quite dark outside now – quite dark and still – and the light in this room is very feeble. It is not a good light for looking carefully at this picture and describing it to you. Besides, I wonder if it would be possible even to make you understand the difference between one kind of painting and another: you might never even have *seen* a painting, in the first few years of your life, and if you did, you probably cannot remember it. I hope, in any case, that the fact you are listening to these words at all means that Gill has found you; which means that this portrait will also now be in your possession, since it forms part of your legacy. So you will at least be able to run your fingers over it, as I am doing now, and feel how thickly Ruth plastered on the paint. It feels rough and scaly, doesn't it? That was her style, always. The especially thick part, at the top of the picture, is your hair. She has used a palette knife to apply layer upon layer of different oranges and golds and yellows. I know I am missing the whole point of the painting when I say this, but my memory, personally, is that your hair wasn't quite as thick and tangled as Ruth has represented it. But I would really need to compare the original photograph that she was working from, and that has no doubt been destroyed.

Your family, you see, would not allow you to come down to Ruth's studio for a proper sitting. She had to work from photographs, which was never her normal way of doing things. That defeated my main object, of course, but no matter. It was only a short-term setback. At least I was in contact with them, now, and it was not long afterwards that I started seeing you again, very occasionally. Altogether we had about three or four meetings, I suppose. Not very much, I know, but I still treasure the memory of every one of them. Anyway, I will come to that in a moment.

The portrait, first. You appear to be sitting astride a wooden fence, which runs diagonally from left to right, in the bottom left-hand corner of the picture. The composition cuts off just above your knees. You are wearing pale green trousers and a dark blue T-shirt. In the photograph it was creamy white, I remember, but Ruth didn't like that colour. The contrast between the rich ultramarine of the T-shirt and your hair is certainly striking. I imagine that was the effect she wanted to achieve. The background is a mottled confusion of different greens, giving a vague suggestion of foliage, with perhaps a hint of whitish sky peeping through. Because of the way you are sitting on the fence, the angle of view is not quite full-frontal, and you are not quite in profile, but somewhere halfway between: what the artists refer to as a three-quarters view, I believe. None the less, your face is turned directly towards the onlooker, and you are smiling: a good, contented smile, which causes your jaw to thrust forward. I suspect that Ruth has exaggerated the size of your jaw, in fact, just as she has exaggerated the thickness of your hair. She had a dislike of pure realism, in literature as well as art.

Certainly this is one of her more accessible paintings. Even in her portrait work – of which she could be rather disdainful, even though it paid a lot of our bills – her take on the visual world was often somewhat skewed. There were several cases of patrons asking for their money back once they saw the results of their commissions. Ruth used to laugh about this, because by the standards of the time, her aesthetic was really very conservative. She was never going to be a fashionable painter. She never won prizes and she was rarely bought by any of the bigger galleries, at least not in this country. Sometimes this made her bitter – especially towards the end of her life. She felt that her work was considered to be too adventurous and difficult by some people, and too conventional by others. Neither one thing nor the other, in other words. I remember her hinting, just before she died, that she was angry with herself for not *letting go* more, for not giving her imagination freer rein: I think she felt that, both in her life and her work, she had been too cautious – hidebound by something, some fear of stepping out of line, of giving offence – something to do with her family background, possibly. Or perhaps it was me, holding her back all that time. I have hardly been one of nature's rebels or mavericks, after all, and despite the fact that Ruth and I never made any secret of our relationship, I made sure that we lived a pretty respectable life in every other way.

Getting back to your portrait (yes, I must get back to that, and quickly), I am sure that it was pressure from me that made her paint it in such a plain and realistic style. What I wanted most of all was that it should simply *look like you*, and in that, of course, she has succeeded quite brilliantly. I love the slight hunch that she has given to your shoulders, suggesting that you are hugging some kind of joyous secret to yourself. That is very characteristic. But what the viewer really notices are your eyes. This is where Ruth has really excelled herself. Everything centres upon your eyes:

your deep blue, sightless eyes that somehow manage to gleam so brightly, with such . . . *energy* in them, such bottomless reserves of wisdom and sadness. Is it not miraculous, how she has managed to capture all that – to capture somebody's *spirit*, to externalize it, to make it permanent and unchanging, using nothing more than a mixture of pigments and vegetable oil? I find it remarkable, what artists can do. 'You have caught her,' I said to Ruth at the time. 'You have caught her exactly.' She did not think very highly of the painting, as I said. 'What do you mean?' she answered. 'It is just a likeness.' That was one of her most damning, dismissive words – 'likeness'. 'No,' I insisted. 'It is more than that. You have said something about Imogen in this picture. *Proved* something about her.' She took issue with that turn of phrase, and asked me exactly what this portrait had 'proved' about you. To which I answered: your *inevitability*.

Let me try to explain what I meant.

As I have mentioned, the painting of this portrait was enough to open a channel of communication with your new family. Shortly after adopting you they had moved south, to Worcester, where there is a very good school for the blind. It was there that I visited you, on a few scattered occasions. My sister's family, including David and Gill, my nephew and niece, lived not far from there, so I had a good pretext for coming to the area. Every few months – not wishing to impose myself, or appear too pushy – I would contact your new father and ask if I might see you, to bring you a little present and perhaps take you out for tea. Do you remember any of that, I wonder, Imogen? Do you remember your strange Aunt Rosamond (although I was never your aunt), who used to collect you from your home and hold you by the hand as we walked along the footpath beside the River Severn, while I described the scene to you? We would sit down on a bench beside the water, and I would tell you all the colours I could see, I would tell you about the curve of the river, about the crows and rooks flying home to their nests in the treetops on the riverbank, about the clothes worn by the people walking past us on their way home from the shops, and the games being played by the schoolboys and schoolgirls on the playing fields opposite. I was so anxious, Imogen, so anxious that you wouldn't *forget* what the world looked like. I was determined to keep your visual sense alive, so that at least you had memories of what you had once seen – strong, vivid memories – even if everything else was now closed to you. And I was succeeding, I'm sure that I was. You listened and you nodded and you understood, I am convinced of it. Just as you will understand – I *have* to believe this, I have to take it on trust, or I will have been wasting my time, all my efforts will have been useless – just as you will understand all the things I have been telling you on these tapes. Am I being foolish, am I being naive again? I don't know, I cannot know. And anyway, it is too late now, everything is too late . . .

I am losing my way again. Perhaps I should not

have any more of this whisky, at least until I have finished this story. It is rather bitter to the taste, but the sensation it imparts is very welcome. So soothing, so calming. I will just take a little drop more ... And now tell you about your mother, the last time I heard from her. It was not long after one of my meetings with you. The portrait was finished by then, I remember, and I stupidly thought that Thea might like to see it. I had been writing to her with news of you, every time I went up to see you, but she hardly ever seemed to reply. With my letter this time, I enclosed a good photographic reproduction of Ruth's portrait. Something else about that letter, I now remember: it was then that I let Thea know your new address. That was wrong of me, no doubt, but not as wrong (or so I thought at the time) as the idea that your mother should be forbidden by law from seeing her own daughter. Anyway, I am quite sure that she never made use of it. A few days later, her reply arrived. An abominable, poisonous letter ... I have never read anything like it, never read anything so twisted or insidious in my life. It was all down to the influence of that man, I am sure, that loathsome Mr Ramsey – whom she had now *married*, for pity's sake – with his wicked perversions of Christian ideas. Somehow, it seems (why on earth am I telling you this? It can do nothing but hurt you) he had managed to persuade Thea that *you*, Imogen – *you*, a blameless, helpless three-year-old girl – had actually been to *blame* for the harm that had befallen you. Your *punishment*, was how she described it: a punishment not inflicted upon you by your mother, apparently, for wetting the bed or whatever it was you were supposed to have done, but handed down by God, working *through* your mother! *That* was how she had come to regard it! I know, I know – at least it is clear to me now – that this was only some kind of . . . psychological mechanism, she was simply trying to exonerate herself – to find a way of *living* with herself – using any means possible, but at the time, the horror and the *fury* that I felt . . . Well. I read the letter only once, I have to say, before screwing it up and throwing it on the fire.

On the mantelpiece above the fire was your newly painted portrait. After reading Thea's letter I stood there and gazed at it for some time. Just as I am gazing at it now. It made me realize, then – and seeing it again just confirms my opinion – that Ruth was a very fine artist indeed. And yes, I will repeat the phrase – it is the inevitability of you that she has captured. When I look at this picture, the whole story runs through my mind – everything I know about Beatrix and her family, from my first encounter with them at Warden Farm in 1941, through her bad marriages and her accident and her neglect and mistreatment of Thea, and then the way your mother grew up feeling unwanted and worthless and in-capable of emotion, and all of these things, all of these things that were so *wrong*, all these unsuitable relationships and bad choices . . . Yes, it was true, none of them should ever have happened, they were all terrible, terrible mistakes, and yet *look what they led to*. They led to you, Imogen! And when I see Ruth's portrait of you, it is obvious that you had to exist. There is such a rightness about you. The notion of your not existing, never having been born, seems so palpably wrong to me, so monstrous and un-natural ... It's not that your existence corrects all of those mistakes, or undoes them. It doesn't *justify* anything. What it means – have I said this before? I think I have, or something like it – or rather, what it makes me understand, is this: that life only starts to make sense when you realize that sometimes – often – all the time – two completely contradictory ideas can be true.

Everything that led up to you was wrong. Therefore, you should not have been born.

But everything about you is right: you *had* to be born.

You were inevitable.

The last picture. The twentieth picture. My fiftieth birthday party.

Fifty glorious years! We had moved to Hampstead by now, Ruth and I, and the party was held in our house there. It was a good day, a happy day, filled with family and friends. The sun shone brightly, and all was well.

You were there too, Imogen. That was my great triumph. I persuaded your family to let you come. And here you are, at the front of the picture. Let me see, now – who else do we have here? Ruth, of course. My sister Sylvia. Both gone now, I'm afraid. Thomas, her husband, was taking the photograph. He is still with us. Must be into his eighties, though. A nice man, an interesting man. You should get him to tell you about his life one day, if you ever meet him. He was a dark horse, Thomas. There was more to him than met the eye. The other person in the picture is Gill. She would have been about twenty-six, twenty-seven. Perhaps I am wrong, but she looks slightly pregnant. She was there by herself, I remember, and seemed a little lost. I don't know why her husband wasn't there, or her brother David. There must have been some reason.

I must describe, describe. And yet I am getting so tired. The story is over now, more or less. Just one or two more things to tell you. Do you really need to know about the clothes we were wearing, the way our hair was parted, the drinks we were holding in our hands? I cannot see that it matters any more. I know it's wrong to give up at this point, so near the end, but . . .

Another drop of whisky, I think. There is still more than half the bottle left.

It was a mistake to invite you. It was lovely having you there, but a mistake. It was all too much for you. So many strangers, strange voices, a strange house for you to find your way around. By the end of the day you were exhausted. Gill was very kind to you, I remember. You recognized a friendly spirit in Gill and clung to her. Unfortunately she and her parents left the party before you did, and your family did not arrive to collect you for about an hour after that. You were very tired.

Here we are, anyway, standing on the steps down to the back garden. The five of us. No Beatrix at this party, of course. We had more or less stopped corresponding by then. Or rather, she had stopped answering my letters. Yes, it was all coming to an end, the whole . . . saga . . .

What happened afterwards was the worst thing,

though. The cruellest blow of all. A letter from your father – your new father, whatever you want to call him – saying that he no longer thought it 'appropriate' that I should have contact with you. He said that you were finding my visits disturbing (whether that was true or not, I have no idea – I very much doubt it), that you had been stressed and agitated following my birthday party, and that it was time to attempt a clean break with your early life. Something he seemed to feel, in his heart of hearts, should have been achieved before. 'In any case,' he added. 'I have been given a placement abroad, and we will soon be leaving the country.' He did not say what he meant by 'abroad', exactly.

I remember that Ruth was working, in those days, in a rented studio a few miles away in East London. On the day I received this letter she returned home late, after dark, and found me sitting at the kitchen table, with the single sheet of paper still in my hand. I told her the news, and it was then, for the first time, that she spoke to me honestly about my relationship with you and Thea and Beatrix. Rosamond, this is for the best, she insisted. It has all gone on for far too long anyway. You owe Beatrix nothing any more. You owe Thea nothing any more. You cannot do anything for this poor little girl. For the time being she is in the care of a good family and when she grows up it will be her own choice whether she wants anything to do with you or not. (You must be thirty years old by now, Imogen, so I suppose you have made that choice.)

For goodness' sake, she insisted, wipe the slate clean. Forget them. Forget all of them.

Well, that was her advice, and very good advice it was too. From her point of view. And well intentioned, certainly. So I took it, as best I could. And from that day onwards I did not write to Beatrix, I did not write to your mother, I did not try to trace you or find out what had become of you. I took all Beatrix's letters and I destroyed them. I took all my photographs of her out of my albums and I put them in a cardboard box and buried them in the attic under piles of junk. Even your portrait, as I have said, went up to Ruth's 'failure room' and was never taken out, never looked at. And the only time, after that, that Beatrix was ever mentioned between us was a few years later when the film *Gone To Earth* was rereleased, and I insisted that Ruth came with me to see it at a cinema near Oxford Street. Which she hated doing, I must say. And I never told her that I had taped it off the television and I never watched that tape until after she had died.

Well, it is not *quite* true, I suppose, that Beatrix was never mentioned again. I forgot that, shortly before Ruth passed away, she did say something about her. To be more precise, she asked me a question.

It might seem odd, but towards the end our relationship became almost entirely silent. Despite living in the same house, and taking all our meals together, and sharing a bed, I don't remember that we spoke to each other much. Hardly at all. What was there to say? We were lifelong companions. We knew each other's opinions, and each other's histories. Or thought that we did, at any rate. If there was anything we didn't care to speak of, we preserved a decent reticence.

During her final illness, though, Ruth did ask me something. I was visiting her in hospital, and although she couldn't walk very well, we had managed to get as far as a bench in one of the little courtyards, which was dominated by a rather ugly concrete water feature. And we had been sitting there for a few minutes when she said to me – most unexpectedly – 'There is something I would like to know about Beatrix.' I looked across at her, and she asked me: 'Was she the one?' I told her that I didn't understand. Ruth said: 'Before me, there was someone else, wasn't there? Someone that you lost. You lost her, and then you settled for me.' I could not meet her eye. I suppose I should have known, all along, that she had understood this, but we had never discussed it, had never mentioned any names, and I swear to you that it had never occurred to me that Ruth might have guessed anything. 'Was it Beatrix?' she asked once more, while I grappled with this new knowledge. After a few seconds I answered: 'No.'

She did not allude to the subject again, after that. And she died just a week or two later.

Rebecca died, too. I saw an announcement placed in one of the newspapers a few months ago. 'Beloved mother,' it said. 'Beloved mother of Peter, Mark and

Sophia.' I had known that already. Not their names, of course, but the fact that she'd married and had children. I saw her by chance in a London restaurant, more than forty years ago. There were four of them sitting around the table – Rebecca, a man, and two little boys – and she also had a tiny baby on her lap. I was supposed to be meeting a friend there and I walked straight in, saw Rebecca and her family, and walked straight out again. Luckily she didn't see me. Her husband did, but he wouldn't have known who I was. I hurried off down the street at a terrific pace and had to telephone my friend later that afternoon to apologize. I was so shaken, so surprised. And angry with her, as well, at the time, although that anger slipped away long ago. After all, if that was the compromise she had decided to make, why not? Who was I to judge, just because I couldn't imagine doing it myself? She had looked happy, very happy. You could see that, at a glance. And probably I was all but forgotten. Me, and Thea, and the two years we had spent together . . .

I say that, but . . .

Perhaps I have been living here too long, all by myself. It used to be that days and days would go by, and I wouldn't have spoken to a soul. More recently, yes, there has been Doctor May – she comes at least twice a week. In fact she will be here tomorrow morning and she will get a surprise, I'm afraid, an unpleasant surprise. I must remember to leave the door unlocked for her . . .

But I have been here too long, and too much alone, there is some truth in that. Sometimes I wonder if I have not been going a little bit mad. Ever since learning that Rebecca died, you see, I have been living with this ... conviction, that ...

No, you will think I am being ridiculous.

But supposing it is true? Supposing she *is* waiting for me somewhere?

Why do I cling to this now, after so many years – a whole lifetime – of not believing?

Is it madness?

I shall tell you what I have come to believe, and you can laugh at me if you will. Inside this house it is cold. And so dark outside, and still. But where she is waiting for me, it will be warm, and the sun will be shining, and the blueness of the sky will be reflected in the waters of the lake. Cerulean blue. And we will be sitting side by side again, in the meadow above the little shingle beach, and she will be leaning into me, and it will be as if the last fifty years have never happened.

How strange, that I should be thinking of her, and of that place, now that the moment has come. I always imagined that my last thought would be of Warden Farm, and Beatrix, the night we became blood-sisters, the night we lay together under the winter moon.

But no. That circle was broken years ago. That was how it all started, yes. Everything followed from that night, but the path it set me upon . . . It was all leading, I realize now, to the day by the lake – *that* was the culmination . . . Everything after that was wrong. When Beatrix came back, to take Thea away, that was when the world tilted, went out of shape . . .

But Imogen exists . . . The rightness of that . . .

Enough. I am going to fetch them now, from the bathroom. And while I'm up, I must check that the back door is unlocked.

Put this microphone . . . somewhere . . .

Right. Here we are. Not quite as many as I thought. Let me . . . tip them out on the table in front of me . . . Almost a dozen. I don't think there should be any problem, in that case . . .

I wonder how quickly they will work. Perhaps I had better put the music on now, just to be sure.

Oh, the stiffness of my joints, these last few weeks!

Now, yes. Soon the violins, and the woodwind. 'Bailero'.

Let it wash over me, while I drink a little more. Not hard to swallow these, after all. Slipping down.

There. Now better hide this somewhere. And the glass.

So, it's done now. No second thoughts.

Ah, this music! The way her voice comes in ... floods everything with light ... like a curtain being drawn back.

Close my eyes now, and I will see it.

Not dark. Not here. Sunlight. Blue. Ceru ...

Oh, I'm going. Much faster than I thought. It's like a cloud, like riding on a cloud.

Someone pulling me.

Darling ...

Are we back now? Soon?

Take my hand. Take it. Pull me towards you.

I see you now.

The lake ...

And a little girl too! Just as I knew it would be.

Oh . . .

Imogen? It's you?

I imagine her now, sitting here beside me on the passenger seat. Imogen, my daughter. Sighted. About to catch her first glimpse of the old farmhouse.

Never to be. In another life, maybe.

Forget these fantasies. Pointless. Pull over to the side of the road.

Windows steamed up. Can't see a thing.

Best get out.

Yes, there it is. And I do remember. Was it really only the one time, that I came here? That Christmas? And yet it feels like coming home.

The shape has changed. Something new has been added. But still, this is the place. Where they lived – my grandparents, my mother. Warden Farm.

Get closer.

Car in the drive. Owners must be at home. How to explain

what I'm doing here? Who are they? Family, my family?
Descendants, cousins? Ivy, my grandmother, died long ago.
Must have. Husband too. Too hard to explain.

Up the drive, just a little way. Beneath the oak. Stood there,
what, forty years ago? More? Christmas night. Smoking.

Someone at the window. Seen me. Watching me now.
Oh God.

Wave. Then back off. Back to the car. Too hard to explain.

Is she coming? No. Mustn't linger, though. Drive on, drive
on quickly.

Where to? Find the village, find the church, find the church-
yard. Find my grandmother again.

*

These Shropshire lanes. Mud everywhere. Burnt umber
hedgerows, dishevelled, wind-battered. Ploughed fields
rolling on either side. Grey sky, looks as if it knows no other
colour. This place feels ancient. Half a century behind the
rest of the world. Feels like nothing has changed since I was
here, nothing.

Now I see the spire. And a pub: Fox and Hounds. Empty car
park. This will do.

*

Nineteen seventy-two, she died. Don't remember anything about it, don't even remember being told. And my grandfather three years later.

Windy spot, this. An easterly wind. Wonder if it's ever quiet, ever silent? Dead of night, maybe? But nowhere silent any more, not in this country. Traffic noise, even here, heart of the countryside. Must be a motorway near by. Wind in the trees, melancholy sound. Makes me think of time. The sound of time passing, implacable.

These graves have been tended, quite recently. Grass trimmed. Someone is looking after them. Need flowers, though. Will buy some, come back tomorrow. Lovely flowers on that one. Narcissus, bright yellow. Somebody cares. Wonder who . . .?

Oh. Oh no.

Rosamond. Last October. Six months ago. Only six months! Only six months too late. Here, though? She ended up here? Must have come back. Come back to where she loved.

Oh no. If only I'd come sooner. Just a word, just a few words. Would have meant so much. To her as well as me.

Footsteps. Who's this?

Man, smiling. Looks friendly. Dog collar. Vicar. Wants to
talk. About to speak to me. Turn. Smile. Get ready.

'Did you know Rosamond, may I ask?'

Thea's letter arrived one morning in late March. Gill was distantly aware of the chatter of well-bred voices from the radio in her father's annexe, but otherwise the house was quiet, and the sudden rattle of the letterbox seemed quite explosive. She went to the front door, a half-slice of toast still lodged between the buttery finger and thumb of one hand, and spotted the letter at once amidst the usual jetsam of bank statements and mobile phone bills. The envelope was blueish, the handwriting erratic and spindly. And it was a thick letter: it felt as though there might be half a dozen pages inside, or even more.

It had arrived sooner than expected. Little more than a week earlier, the Reverend Tawn had phoned her with some startling, but welcome news: walking home through the churchyard on a blustery weekday afternoon, he had come upon a gaunt, angular woman with time- and weatherbeaten features, probably in her late fifties, standing over Rosamond's grave and reading the inscription on the headstone with distress in her eyes. A few minutes' halting conversation had established that this was none other than Thea, Beatrix's daughter, newly returned to the country after many years away. He had invited her into the vicarage, sat her down, given her tea and told her all that he knew about Rosamond's final illness and death. She had listened with keen interest – fascination, even – and, on learning of Gill's role as executor, had asked to be put in touch with her at once.

'I wasn't sure if I should give her your number,' the vicar had explained over the phone that evening. 'So I simply took her address instead. Would you like to have it? She's eager to hear from you.'

Gill had written to Thea the very next day; telling her all about the tapes to which she had listened with her daughters (although she omitted, for now, the details of how they had ended) and describing their hitherto fruitless search for Imogen. A search which might now, she hoped, with this new discovery, be coming to an end.

Gill tossed the other envelopes impatiently on to one of the kitchen work surfaces and sat down at the table with Thea's letter. Sunlight spilled over the domestic clutter, the breakfast debris, spun back and reflected by the glass panels of the conservatory beyond the kitchen windows. Outside it was a stubbornly cold spring morning, and dew still lay thick on the lawn, pale and glimmering. Gill had been about to shower and put some warm clothes on, but that could wait now. She slit the envelope open with a butter knife, spent a moment or two adjusting her gaze to the difficult, unfamiliar handwriting, and then began to read, her eyes darting and eager.

Thank you [Thea had begun] for your very full and friendly letter.

To be honest, I'd forgotten about the portrait of Imogen. Forgotten that it even existed. There's so much from that time that I've forgotten – or maybe blotted out. It's a quarter of a century ago, after all! And sometimes seems even longer, to me. But anyway – good to know that you have it. I'd love to come over and see it some time, if you'll let me.

As for what you told me about the tapes Rosamond left behind, I am simply amazed. So you've heard them, and you know the whole story. I don't know how that makes me feel – slightly uncomfortable, I suppose – but pleased that you still wanted to write. Some people, when they learn about what happened back then, find it hard to forgive me – or even treat me as a normal human being. So I'm very grateful to you, for not being like that. I take a lot of comfort from it. Especially as you are (however distantly) family, and family is the most important thing in my life. Perhaps you will think that a peculiar thing for me, of all people, to say, but I think from the tone of your letter that you'll understand what I mean. I hope so.

Now, there's something that I owe you in return: news of Imogen. It's quite a long story, which I want to tell you from the beginning. So please be patient with me and try not to mind if I start rambling here and there.

I suppose the place to begin is the time when Rosamond and I quarrelled and broke off contact.

After coming out of prison I made the mistake of marrying the wrong man. His name was Derek Ramsey, and he was very cruel and controlling. Altogether I was with him for about ten years. He'd seen my picture in the newspaper before my trial and he'd written to me while I was in prison. He belonged to a small and peculiar offshoot of the Mormon Church, and something about my situation had struck a chord with him. He had all sorts of theories about why I'd done what I did to Imogen: they all boiled down to the idea that Satan was within her, and what had happened to her was some kind of punishment that she deserved. I was in such a desperate state in those days, and so full of guilt, that I managed to tell myself that I believed him. It was a horrible, horrible lie, but I can see now that it must have made me feel better, given me some way of being able to live with myself after what I'd done.

The years went by, and our life together became more and more intolerable. Slowly, some little spark of independence, and humanity, that must always have been glowing inside me reignited itself and burst into flame. I left my husband, and I've never seen him since.

The main thing that kept me going during this time was an incredible, almost overpowering desire to see Imogen again. By the time I left Derek, she would have been about sixteen years old. I didn't want to disrupt her new life in any way. I just wanted to see her and know that she was happy.

Rosamond had once given me an address for my daughter's new family, and that was where I went.

They had moved on, long ago, but fortunately the current residents of the house had been left with a forwarding address. It was an address in Toronto.

I took this as a very hopeful sign. My mother had also moved to Canada, and although we hadn't been in touch for many years, I'd also recently had the idea of going out there to see her. It seemed that fate (not God – I didn't believe in Him any more) was deliberately pointing a finger towards Canada and telling me to go there. So I booked my plane ticket and left.

I arrived in Toronto, checked into a motel on the outskirts of the city, and the very next day I hired a car and drove over to where Imogen's family lived and parked right opposite their house. Of course this was a risky thing to do because I wasn't really allowed to have any contact with her. It was a Sunday morning. I stayed there for a few hours and just before lunchtime they all came out and got into their car. You have to remember that I hadn't set eyes on my daughter since she was three years old, and I wasn't at all sure that I'd even recognize her. However, I have to say that the white stick was a bit of a giveaway! Even without it, though, there would have been no mistaking my Imogen. She had grown up very tall and beautiful, with her blonde hair cut into a nice bob, and she carried herself very gracefully. There were two other children besides her – younger children, two boys – and a big brown Irish terrier who they all made a lot of fuss of. You could easily tell that they were a close and happy family.

The next day I came back first thing in the morning

and watched as Imogen got into the car with her mother. I followed the car as they drove off to school. It seemed that she was just attending a normal high school near the city centre, not a special school for the blind. That afternoon I waited outside the school entrance, but Imogen was picked up by her mother, and there was no opportunity to speak to her. In any case I had no idea what I was going to say! The same thing happened the next day. But on the next afternoon, the Wednesday, I was in luck and I saw her come out through the gates by herself, and walk down to the bus stop a few hundred yards down the road. I walked to the bus stop behind her, and I got on the same bus as she did. I was amazed by how easily she did everything, how she seemed to know the exact position of the doors and the height of the steps and everything like that. People kept taking her by the arm and trying to help her, but she didn't really need it.

The bus was crowded and a gentleman got up to give her his seat. She sat down and I found that I was standing in the aisle right next to her. I stood there like that for almost fifteen minutes, until we both got off. It was an incredible feeling, being so close to my lovely daughter again. As we got off the bus, I actually took her arm and helped her down the step. Actually touched her. And she said, 'Thank you, ma'am.' I don't know how she knew I was a woman not a man.

We were at a stop near the university, now, and she walked to the front entrance of what looked like an imitation of an old Oxford or Cambridge college. There was a boy waiting for her there – a student who I suppose was about nineteen or twenty – and the two of them kissed on the steps. I noticed how she ran her fingers over his face, around his chin and down his neck. He was a very good-looking boy and I could see that she liked the touch of him. He took her by the arm and they went for a walk in the park near by – Queen's Park, I believe it's called. I followed them at a distance, at first, but then I began to get worried and self-conscious. Also I was feeling very agitated after touching her, and hearing her speak to me. My heart was going nineteen to the dozen. So I took the bus back to my motel room and lay down for a while.

The next day, her mother picked her up in the car again. But on Friday afternoon Imogen went back to the bus stop after school, and once more I followed her.

This time luck was even more on my side. She was early for her meeting with the boyfriend, so she went to Queen's Park by herself, and sat down on a bench to wait. She was wearing a grey herringbone coat and pale blue jeans, and she left her stick resting against the bench beside her while she tilted her face back and enjoyed the feel of the sun and the breeze. It was autumn: lovely weather – cold and crisp. She had a half-smile on her face. I wished she could have seen the leaves on the trees and on the grass all around her. They were absolutely beautiful – every shade of green, yellow, red and brown you could imagine. There were lots of big grey squirrels running about between the leaves. I remember them, for some reason.

I'd already worked out what I was going to do. I took the cashmere scarf from around my neck and sat down beside her and said, 'Excuse me, is this yours?' She put out her hands and felt it and said, 'A scarf. No, it's not mine. Did somebody drop it?' I told her I'd found it on the path and then I said, 'Do you mind if I sit here?' and she said no she didn't, and then before I'd even had the chance to think how I was going to keep the conversation going, she saved me the trouble, by asking: 'You're English, aren't you?' She had noticed my English accent, and suddenly for the first time it occurred to me that she might even recognize my voice. But I don't think she did. It was all such a long time ago, after all.

There was so much I wanted to say to her, so much I wanted to ask, but we didn't have much time, and I couldn't be too direct. Instead, all I could do was make small talk with her, as if she were a stranger. Most of the time we talked about the differences between Canada and England. She said that she remembered England well, even though she hadn't been back for nearly eight years. She said that she could remember the dampness and the greyness of it, and I asked her – without meaning to be rude – how she could talk about the greyness of it when she couldn't see; and she said that although she'd lost her sight very young, she could still remember what the world looked like. She could still remember shapes and colours. Trying to keep my voice from trembling, I asked her how she had come to be blind; but when she replied, she didn't say anything about me, as such: just that there had been a bad accident, and she couldn't remember much about it. And then she said something I remember very well: that she knew what people thought – that because she was blind, her life must be terribly sad and difficult – but she didn't feel it was like that at all. So far, she said, her life had been as happy and as rich and as full as anybody else's. Which was a wonderful thing for me to hear, as I'm sure you can well believe.

Much too soon, I could see her boyfriend coming towards us; and at the same moment, she said, 'Ah, here he is' – because she'd heard his footsteps, and obviously recognized them. She got up and they kissed again and once more he took her by the arm and off they went together. But not before she'd wished me goodbye, and said that it was 'Nice talking to you, ma'am.' As they went, I could hear him asking her, 'Who was that?' but I didn't hear what she answered. I sat on the bench and watched them until they were out of sight. It was a clear afternoon, and because Imogen's hair was so blonde you could make them out for a long time.

After that, I had nothing more to do in Toronto. I'd found my daughter again and I could see that she was well and happy, and she was being well cared for. I knew now that as soon as she was eighteen I would write to her family and ask if I could see her again. That day was more than a year away and it seemed an awful long time to wait, but I felt I could probably manage it, having seen her and spoken to her this one time.

So off I went to see my mother. I knew that she was unwell. She had cancer of the throat and she was spending most of her time in hospital, now. In fact she passed away just four weeks after my meeting with Imogen. I saw her several times before she died. It would be nice to say that we made up all our differences, and that everything was made good again between us. That would have given me 'closure', as I believe the psychologists call it. But I'm afraid my mother remained cantankerous and critical right up until the end. The plain fact is that she never really liked me, and never wanted me. I had been a mistake; and that, to some extent, is what I remain in my own eyes, to this day. The knowledge never goes, can never be undone. You just have to find a way to live with it.

During this time I was staying with my half-sister, Alice. I'd never had much time for her, when we were children – the age difference had always seemed too great – but now I could see what a kind and good person she'd become. And I suppose we bonded, of course, over the death of our mother. Anyway, it was Alice who persuaded me to stay on in Canada. I settled down there and got myself a part-time job and ended up staying there for the next fourteen years. After Mum died my stepfather Charles never remarried, and towards the end of his life he needed quite a bit of looking after, so I was at least able to make myself useful there. He died last year and that's really why I've come back to England; I suppose there was nothing left for me to do in Canada. That, and a little bit of homesickness, although I don't really have anything to be homesick for.

You must still be wondering about Imogen. I wish I had something good to tell you. But when I did finally pluck up the courage to write to her family, they wrote back with some dreadful news. Imogen died. She died in a road accident, of all things. It was the school holidays, and she was out in the park with her brothers one morning, taking that dog for a walk. And apparently, although it had never done anything like this before, the dog suddenly ran off, barking, into the road, and Imogen heard him and ran off after him. Such a dangerous thing to do, but I don't suppose she was thinking. *He* managed to dodge all the traffic, and landed up safe and sound on the other side of the road: but she was hit by a car. She didn't have a chance, poor girl. It happened in a flash. She wouldn't have felt anything. It was one week before her seventeenth birthday, and almost six months to the day after I'd seen her in Toronto. April 16th, 1992. The day my daughter died.

How do you console yourself when something like that happens? For months I was in a sort of denial, trying . . .

There were only a few lines left, but Gill read no more. The last page dropped on to the table as she sat back, despondent, and her fingers loosened their grip on the paper.

She gazed ahead of her for perhaps a minute or more, unable to think, her powers of reasoning all but crushed by the weight of the sudden disappointment bearing down upon her.

Then scattered thoughts began shooting through her mind, rapidly, at random.

A dog that ran away, inexplicably. First Beatrix in pursuit, then Imogen. Grandmother and granddaughter, almost fifty years apart . . .

The Auvergne: Rosamond imagining that she would arrive there when she died. Gill herself travelling there with her husband, and then driving alone along an empty road. A blackbird thudding into her windscreen, a horrible intimation of death . . .

When was that? 1992? April? It had happened in the afternoon, late in the afternoon. Imogen had died in the morning. Toronto . . . France . . . What was the time difference?

Nothing was random, after all. There was a pattern: a pattern to be found somewhere . . .

Then she was startled out of her chair by the telephone's ringing. Caller display told her that it was Elizabeth. She grabbed the handset from its cradle on the wall.

'Hello, love? Is everything OK?'

'Yes, Mum, I'm fine. I just wondered if Catharine had called you yet.'

'Catharine? No. Why should Catharine call me?'

'Oh, you haven't heard.' A pause. 'Daniel left her.'

'Oh, no.'

'He told her last night.'

'Oh, poor Catharine.'

'She came round to my place at about ten, crying

her eyes out. I let her stay the night here. She's gone back now and she said she was probably going to call you . . . Mum, are you still there?'

'Yes, I'm still here.'

'Are *you* OK?'

'Yes, only . . . Only, I've had some news today as well.'

'What sort of news?'

'It's fine, love, really. I'll call you again later. Is that all right? I'll call you in about half an hour. I'd better get off the line, your sister might be trying to get through.'

Gill hung up and stood in the centre of the kitchen, giddy, her thoughts still spiralling. A patchwork, made up of . . . coincidences? Was that what they were? If only she could stand back, see the design more clearly. But if anything it was getting fainter, already. From far away, far off in London, Catharine's sense of loss and abandonment was transmitting itself, stealing into her mother's heart, freighted with anger as well as pain. That bastard Daniel . . . She had *known*, she had known all along that he would do something like this . . .

But no . . . *Don't let the present wipe out the past.* Not yet. The answer was there, it was there for the finding. Surely she was being offered something precious beyond belief, some supreme revelation. There was *meaning* in all this . . .

The phone rang again. Caller display told her that it was Catharine this time. Gill waited, waited just a few more seconds before picking up and in that stretched instant she felt the promise of revelation curl, evaporate and vanish; watched in despair as it slipped for ever through her mind's grasping fingers. Even before she heard her daughter's first, broken words, she knew that it was too late. The pattern she had been searching for had gone. Worse than that – it had never existed. How could it? What she had been hoping for was a figment, a dream, an impossible thing: like the rain before it falls.

JONATHAN COE

THE TERRIBLE PRIVACY OF MAXWELL SIM

'Clever, engaging, spring-loaded with mysteries and surprises. Hugely enjoyable' *Time Out*

'Classic Coe' *Vogue*

Maxwell Sim could be any of us. He could be you.

He's about to have a mid-life crisis (though he doesn't know it yet). He'll be found in his car in the north of Scotland, half-naked and alone, suffering hypothermia, with a couple of empty whiskey bottles and a boot full of toothbrushes.

It's a far cry from a restaurant in Sydney, where his story starts.

But then Maxwell Sim has, unknowingly, got a long way to go. If he knew now about the toothbrushes, or the dead man on the aeroplane, or his father and the folded photograph, or Poppy the Adultery Facilitator, or even about Emma's lovely, fading voice, then perhaps he'd stay where he was – hiding from his destiny.

But Max knows none of it. And nor do you – at least not yet . . .

'Witty, unexpected and curiously unsettling' *Literary Review*

'Unceasingly enjoyable' *Prospect*

Jonathan Coe

THE HOUSE OF SLEEP

'Hilarious and devastating' *The Times*

A group of students share a house in the '80s, fall in and out of love, and drift apart.

A decade later they are drawn back together by a series of coincidences involving their obsession with sleep. Sarah is a narcoleptic who has dreams so vivid she mistakes them for real events; Robert has his life changed for ever by the misunderstandings that arise from her condition; Terry, the insomniac, spends his wakeful nights fuelling his obsession with movies; and the increasingly unstable Dr Gregory Dudden sees sleep as a life-shortening disease which he must eradicate …

'Moving as well as clever, pleasurable as well as smart … it must be one of the best books of the year' *The Times*

'A remarkable book … not only a clever novel, but also one that creates a powerful, hypnotic emotional intensity … Perhaps most strange of all, for a novel about insomniacs, *The House of Sleep* is a wonderful bedtime read' *Sunday Times*

'This is a fiercely clever, witty novel, but it is also wise, generous and hopeful … Coe has been compared to Peacock, Waugh and Wodehouse, but this novel shows he has outgrown even this distinguished lineage. A compellingly beautiful tale of love and loss' *The Times Literary Supplement*

'Energy, tenderness, social commitment, all in a style that comes like breath … one of the very best contemporary British novelists' *Independent on Sunday*

JONATHAN COE

EXPO 58

'Hilarious, brilliant, compelling' *Observer*

The World's Fair, Belgium, 1958. Freshly arrived is mild-mannered civil servant Thomas Foley, here to ensure the British contribution – a pub called the Britannia – is no national embarrassment. But it is the height of the Cold War and the Fair is a hotbed of paranoia and deceit. With his superiors fearful of leaked secrets and defections, Thomas is spied on and directed to spy on others. Thrust into a game he barely understands, distracted by a romance which tests his marital and family loyalties to their limit, Thomas gamely tries to do the right thing – if only someone will tell him what that is . . .

'Top notch, rollicking, more than a clever comedy' *Literary Review*

'A comico-serious delight, absorbs from start to finish' *Evening Standard*

'Clever and funny, enthralling and moving' *Daily Mail*

'Delightfully funny and utterly absurd. Tremendously good fun' *Spectator*

'Coe at his funny-serious best. Pure enjoyment' *Financial Times*

He just wanted a decent book to read ...

Not too much to ask, is it? It was in 1935 when Allen Lane, Managing Director of Bodley Head Publishers, stood on a platform at Exeter railway station looking for something good to read on his journey back to London. His choice was limited to popular magazines and poor-quality paperbacks – the same choice faced every day by the vast majority of readers, few of whom could afford hardbacks. Lane's disappointment and subsequent anger at the range of books generally available led him to found a company – and change the world.

'We believed in the existence in this country of a vast reading public for intelligent books at a low price, and staked everything on it'
Sir Allen Lane, 1902–1970, founder of Penguin Books

The quality paperback had arrived – and not just in bookshops. Lane was adamant that his Penguins should appear in chain stores and tobacconists, and should cost no more than a packet of cigarettes.

Reading habits (and cigarette prices) have changed since 1935, but Penguin still believes in publishing the best books for everybody to enjoy. We still believe that good design costs no more than bad design, and we still believe that quality books published passionately and responsibly make the world a better place.

So wherever you see the little bird – whether it's on a piece of prize-winning literary fiction or a celebrity autobiography, political tour de force or historical masterpiece, a serial-killer thriller, reference book, world classic or a piece of pure escapism – you can bet that it represents the very best that the genre has to offer.

Whatever you like to read – trust Penguin.